High Heels & S...

A Jackson's ...

Boo...

Grace Harper

Ingrid and Harvey

Chapter 1

The 16th Century manor house had been the home of Ingrid Stellar for a year. She'd bought the house for cash, much to the surprise of the estate agent. The man took a long gaze at Ingrid, came to a conclusion, and didn't ask any further questions. For a moment, Ingrid wanted to quiz him on what he had assumed, what assumptions he had made that meant she could afford a six hundred-thousand-pound house, with no mortgage. The urge lasted a minute and a half until she realised she didn't give a fuck what he thought. She'd never have to see him again once the house keys were in her hands.

The pretty, pale brick house stood alone on the outskirts of a small town in Surrey. A river ran along the bottom of her garden. She would often sit on the wooden bench she'd built to feed the ducks. The house allowed for a mooring for a small boat, but she'd sold the one that came with the house. She had no desire to be on the water in a boat or a ship.

Until recently, Ingrid hadn't spent more than three days in a row in the house since she'd bought it. Her job kept her busy, flying around the world. She had experienced the best in luxury travel that money could buy for the last ten years. Her career as a high-end escort had afforded her anything she wanted. Her dates gave more than money to be their escort. She owned so much jewellery that she couldn't wear it all. Clothing, accessories, and shoes cluttered her wardrobes. Ingrid had been gifted cars, and one of her hosts bought her an apartment in central London. The most generous of the men she escorted, she'd never even kissed. They wanted a professional, and she enjoyed being just that.

Ingrid had spent the best part of the afternoon pottering around her home, a few weeks after her final date in Hong Kong. The first week flew by with long lazy lie ins and late-night movie watching. The second week, Ingrid mooched around the house, deciding what she would do with each room. When she'd bought the property, there were no repairs needed, but it wasn't decorated in line with her style. Each time she had planned to paint the walls, her Madam had called, and then she packed her bags and flew to her next date.

Travelling the world in luxury had become tedious, it wasn't on her terms. The number of times she had arrived in a foreign country, been whisked away in a limo only to be escorted back three days later, having never left the hotel suite. Ingrid was paid extremely well for that timetable, but once in a while, she would have wanted to do a little sightseeing.

By the third week, Ingrid was getting used to having her time back, she had spring cleaned the entire house in the middle of summer. Preparing the house to be lived in properly was the focus of her days and evenings. Her next task would be to convert the back bedroom into a study to make a start on her first novel.

As a reward for working hard, washing and scrubbing down the walls in the upstairs spare room, Ingrid had walked into the local town to eat a slice of cake from her favourite cafe. Her mind had wandered to all the plans she had for the future. The shrill of her mobile phone startled her into the real world.

Her daydreams of sitting on a Parisian street scribbling away were rudely interrupted.

"I know you said that you were finished and last month was your last appointment," Ingrid's Madam said. "I'd like you to take one more client, as a favour," she said. "You're about to say no, but don't."

Ingrid's Madam never greeted her when she called, she hated any pleasantries and small talk. Ingrid wondered what her Madam looked like. She imagined a sixty-year-old with greying, wiry hair. In her mind, she always pictured her in a green tweed skirt and jacket with a high collared white blouse.

"Good afternoon, beautiful weather we've been having," Ingrid said. She always tried to get her Madam to break from the usual business talk. When no reply came, Ingrid answered her Madam. "Do I have a choice?"

"Not for this kind of money, my cut will be enormous," she said. Her Madam was over excited at the prospect of earning so much money for a single booking.

Ingrid, opened mouthed, ready with the word no on the tip of her tongue, paused to see what was on offer. She closed her lips without saying a word. From her window seat in the cafe, she inspected the mother and four unruly children outside on the pavement. The kids were laughing, running around in circles blowing bubbles from the wand in their hands. Ingrid's chest ached for a moment, ached for the chance of having children.

"Tell me about him," Ingrid said. Her eyes were still glued to the family scene. The mother looked tired but happy, pulling a tissue out of her Mary Poppins handbag, then catching the youngest child and wiping his nose. Ingrid heard the sigh of relief on the other end of the phone, and then her Madam launched into the brief.

"He's a wealthy man, magazines and other editorials. The fourth generation to handle the company but he's a bit of a recluse these days. Married twice but they didn't last long, he loved them by all accounts, but the women just wanted his money," she said.

Ingrid grunted at the last comment and waved at one of the girls as the bubbles floated towards the window, leaving a soapy residue as it burst.

"How old is he?" Ingrid asked.

"Forty-Five, fit as fuck, you'll have a great time with him," she said.

"If you say so, what's his name?" Ingrid asked. The family had gone, and she now stared at the cooling mug of coffee on the laminate tabletop. The cafe attracted the workmen and truckers of the area. The tea was the colour of a bad fake tan, and the breakfast was cardiac arrest worthy. The cafe was her guilty pleasure. If she knew she had a week off, Ingrid would come to the cafe for sticky buns and decadent cake.

"Harvey Hinder," she said.

Ingrid's heart paused for a fraction of a second, the mug she was holding near her lips stopped in its tracks. She moved the cup back to the table and closed her eyes.

"Say his name again, it's a bit noisy this end," Ingrid said. She looked around the empty cafe, even the staff were out back playing cards until the next customer came in.

"Harvey, Hinder," her Madam barked.

"Never heard of him, I'll do my research," Ingrid said, never faltering in her speech. "Send me the details. I'm assuming its regular rates?"

"No. He's offering quadruple the price. He wants you for five days, ending at a party next Saturday, but he said that's optional. He'd like you to attend the party with him only if you want to and not because he's paying you."

"Did you just quote Pretty Woman?"

"Focus, Ingrid," she barked. "He wants to pick you up on Monday and drive you to his home. He knows that you'll have to rearrange appointments and has said he isn't expecting twenty-four seven attention. If you can't get out of anything you've arranged next week, he says he's okay with it. But he gets you from 5pm to 11am, no matter what."

"I've made plans next week, in Brighton, I can't stay in London. Plus I have my own party next Saturday to attend. I can't get out of that," Ingrid said.

"Is it the *Ipris* Gala, by any chance?"

"Yes, it is, why?"

"Harvey owns *Ipris*, it's his party," she said. "His home is in Brighton, or just outside, a place called Jackson's Bay."

Ingrid closed her eyes once more, attempting to calm her beating heart. Spending one on one time with Harvey sent her nerve endings on fire.

Ingrid wanted to yell down the phone that she would absolutely take the job. She would have waived her fee to spend the week with Harvey. Not only did Ingrid admire his business acumen, but she found him extremely attractive. occasionally, Ingrid and Harvey had been at the same party. The opportunity for them to be introduced had never occurred as he rarely spent more than fifteen minutes at any social occasion. Those minutes were enough for her to know that she was drawn to him, fascinated by the man who exuded charm and charisma without the outward arrogance. His genial smile warmed her heart. Her fantasies had included him on more than a few occasions. What puzzled her, was why a hot, rich, brilliant man would need an escort. She assumed that Harvey had a girlfriend but kept his relationship quiet. She didn't question why she was hired by hugely successful men but wanted to know why this man wanted to hire her.

The arrangement could work. Ingrid could meet with Rebecca and her other friends during the day and spend time with Harvey in the evenings. She did have a date for the party, another of her escort colleagues, Lucas, was going with her. They'd agreed they'd go together if they didn't find dates. Ingrid would tell Lucas he was on his own. There was no way she was giving up the chance to attend a gala party with Harvey, even if he only stayed for fifteen minutes.

Ingrid was all in.

"Okay, it'll work, I'll do it. This is the last one, Madam, the very last. You gotta have a goal. Do you have a goal?"

"Now who's quoting Pretty Woman," she said, and ended the call.

Pushing the cold mug of coffee away, Ingrid left the cafe calling out her goodbyes as she pushed open the door and donned her sunglasses.

Chapter 2

I ngrid's Madam had sent her the details for the week in Jackson's Bay. On Sunday evening at 8pm, a car service would arrive to collect her suitcases and take them to Harvey's home. On Monday morning, another car service would come at 10am to take her to Jackson's Bay and to his home. The driver arrived in full livery at exactly 8pm yesterday. The curl of excitement twisted in Ingrid's belly at the prospect of a week with Harvey. When her Madam told her that Harvey was fit as fuck, she already knew this. A man can't disguise a healthy body under a suit any more than hiding extra pounds. The photographs the media took of the man were flawless, his relaxed manner and smile told anyone who viewed them that he was confident in all things.

Ingrid glanced at the clock one more time to see that she had another hour to wait. Kicking off her nude coloured wedges, Ingrid slumped into the armchair nearest the window that would have a full view of her drive. Anyone approaching her front door via foot or car could be seen from this seat.

Her beauty routine had started hours ago with a long hot bath. On Saturday for the gala ball, she would have a glam squad to get her camera ready, but until then she prepared her body and face herself. Years of practice and lessons had taught her every kind of beauty regime. Her clients wanted what they paid for, and that was a highly polished, sexy woman on their arm. She assumed Harvey would be no different, especially as he'd pulled her out of retirement, paying her a small fortune for the week. The least she could do was make an effort. She allowed the truth to seep through her mind and that was she would have made an effort even if she did spend time with him free of charge.

Her phone chirped in her handbag on the table in the hallway. Hauling her body up from the comfortable armchair, she peered at the screen of her work phone. Her personal phone stayed silent at the bottom of the bag.

Harvey: Your driver has arrived early. Shall I send him away until 10am or are you ready to go?

Harvey had asked for her number via her Madam and Ingrid had agreed. For a week's job, she needed to have contact with him. For her single evening dates, Ingrid didn't disclose her number, once the date was over, she didn't want to hear from them again. Some of the men she dated wanted more and changing her number every time that happened would have become a pain. Her Madam filtered all calls and texts and passed on what was important or relevant. This time her Madam had encouraged Ingrid to give out her number. She reasoned it was her final job and she could always toss the phone once the week was over.

Ingrid: Don't send him away, I'm ready, give me five minutes to lock up the house.

"Showtime," Ingrid said to the empty house.

Slipping her shoes back on, she walked through the ground floor checking the doors and windows. Once they were all secure, she stepped backwards out of her front door with her cute beige handbag and pulled her wooden front door shut. Placing a palm on the door just above the lock she whispered a promise to the house she would spend more time within its walls soon.

When she turned a gust of wind blew up the flared summer skirt of her dress, and she was sure her driver caught a glimpse of her shapely tanned legs and possibly her red lace underwear. The quiet beep of the horn snapped her head around to the car in the drive. A flustered man glared at his steering wheel, looking like he was blaming the car for sounding the horn and not his fingers when they gripped the steering wheel.

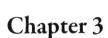

Chapter 3

Harvey had misjudged where the horn was when he saw Ingrid's dress rise up in a true Marilyn Monroe pose. His thumb grabbed the button that made the noise by mistake, he pulled it away like he'd been electrocuted, hoping his guest hadn't heard. When he dragged his eyes up from her legs to her face, and their eyes locked he knew he was busted. Her smirk let him know.

He commanded dozen of companies, making millions of pounds, year in year out and the sight of Ingrid's legs sent him straight back to adolescence. He had stepped out of the car before he banged his head on the dashboard with embarrassment to meet the woman he hoped would see past the public profile and learn about the real Harvey Hinder.

As he strode the few yards to Ingrid, he glimpsed the subtle widening of her eyes. He was glad that Ingrid's Madam hadn't revealed he would be driving her to Jackson's Bay. He didn't want to catch her off guard, he aimed to not give her any excuses of backing out of the personal driver. He imagined she was used to being driven to her date by any amount of strangers but this week was personal and no one would be driving her anywhere but him.

"Hello," he said. "I'm Harvey, it's great to meet you, Ingrid," Harvey said extending his arm out to shake her hand. He'd never been so formal with a woman he wanted in his bed. If it were any other woman, he would have kissed her cheek in greeting. At the moment, he was pretending she was a businesswoman, and they were going to discuss an amalgamation of two companies.

"Hi, I'm delighted to meet you. I had no idea I would be driven by you, I was expecting a driver service like last night," she said and took his hand in greeting.

He held her hand moments longer than etiquette dictated. He found that he was gently pulling her closer. Ingrid complied and stepped closer until their clasped hands were the only thing separating them. They'd naturally bent their elbows to stand close. Harvey's eyes darted from her eyes to her lips, making a decision. After a few beats, he leaned in and kissed her cheek, planting his lips on her soft skin for a few seconds. When he withdrew and dropped her hand, he saw the pink colour rise in her cheeks, giving Ingrid the look of a perfect English rose.

"I wouldn't hear of a stranger driving you, I will take care of you this week. Apart from a housekeeper, it will be just us," Harvey said. "You might bump into my brother, but that is not yet confirmed." He added. He didn't know why he was saying all of this, he couldn't keep his cool. He was embarrassed that he wasn't in control around her.

To avoid any more talking, he led her to the passenger seat of his ruby red sports car, placing the flat of his hand lightly at the base of her back. Her cream summer dress was high to the neck, fitted at the torso but the back dipped low to her waist. He risked a touch of her skin and relished in the involuntary shiver from Ingrid. He knew then and there that she was attracted to him and not just because she was paid to be. His hopes soared at that point. All doubt was eradicated. A woman

like her wouldn't blush as a chaste kiss and shiver at an inno-
cent touch. She wanted to be with him.

"Will we be driving to many places this week?" Ingrid
asked.

She'd settled into the low seat. The tinted windows pre-
vented Harvey from seeing too much while he rounded the
front of the car, but he didn't take his eyes off her silhouette
as she pulled her seatbelt across her body and into place. He
dropped into the driver's seat, strapping himself in and started
the ignition.

"We can go wherever you want to go. I'm hoping we can
enjoy each other's company this week. Explore the area, eat
well, and relax. I rarely get the opportunity to slow my life
down. We can look at a map of the area and decide where we
want to go over dinner this evening."

Harvey watched her reaction, taking in her pursed lips and
the crinkle between her eyebrows. A slow smile graced her full,
beautifully painted lips and when she turned to look at him, he
was arrested with the intensity behind her eyes.

"Sounds fantastic," she said.

When Ingrid didn't say anything further, slipping down a
little in her seat to get comfortable, he reversed out of her drive and out onto the main village road. He couldn't wait to start
their week.

Chapter 4

When Ingrid arrived in Jackson's Bay, a couple of days ago, sitting in the passenger seat of Harvey's sports car, she'd stared open mouthed at the house looming up out of the trees. Their journey up the gravel dirt road to the most ostentatious mansion she had ever seen, put her pile of bricks into insignificance. The building would be her home for the next five days. She couldn't get over the fact that he had picked her up personally. The driver was the reclusive media mogul. They had discussed on the journey down to Jackson's Bay her appointments for the week. He didn't pry when she didn't reveal who she was meeting.

Ingrid had met with the Editor-in-Chief the day before, while it had gone better than she'd expected, she didn't think telling Harvey who she was meeting was a good idea. Giving up her column at the magazine was a hard decision to make, but she wanted to walk away from her escort life in its entirety.

The column she wrote for *Ipris* was an insight to escort life, the glamour side of making money as a professional date. She also wrote about the quirks that her clients wanted. The stories ended when she said goodnight. Ingrid didn't see herself as a prostitute, and that was what she tried to articulate in her column each month. It was a matter of perspective.

After ten years in the business, Ingrid was set for life, financially. One night dates with the wealthy and famous no longer held the allure it once did. To soften the blow to Rebecca, Ingrid offered the story telling services of her colleague, a young male escort called Lucas. He would take over the column as a fresh take on the subject of professional dating services. Rebecca had loved the idea when they'd met yesterday. She received an email later that night to say that she would take on Lucas as a feature writer, but it would be restricted to online only and behind a smoke screen that subscribers paid for.

Ingrid's mind wandered to the past as she grew bored waiting for Harvey to finish his conference call in the study. Lunch had arrived soon after they returned from a drive along the coast an hour ago. The food was gently warming in the blistering heat of the day. Ingrid was tempted to tell her client that she wrote a column for his magazine, to see the shocked look on his face. Rebecca might have been her boss and editor-in-chief of the magazine, but Harvey owned the worldwide media franchise. In theory, she no longer worked for him and could tell him, but she'd kept her secret this long it would be foolish to spoil a perfectly good week. The more people who knew, the more chance that she would be recognised in her everyday life. Her plans of a quiet existence were mapped out in her head, and a confession was not on the cards.

Harvey Hinder was a wealthy businessman whose family had been in the newspaper and magazine industry for over two hundred years. He was old money without the arrogance to match. Ingrid had been told by Rebecca that no one knew who she was. Her pen name bore no resemblance to her proper name. Many people had tried over the years to find out who the mystery writer was and hadn't succeeded. Several fake women had come forward claiming that they were the infamous writer at *Ipris* Magazine. Each time it was proven that they were lying and out to cash in on Ingrid's success. She put it down to co-incidence that she sat in the living room of a stunning mansion with her soon to be ex-boss. Her research had revealed that Harvey had given up on relationships after his second wife left him. It was worldwide news when he dated, married, or divorced. According to the press, he hadn't dated in many years, favouring business instead.

Spending the week in luxury and getting paid day and night to be with Harvey was just fine with Ingrid. Harvey's charisma matched his good looks, but he was also smart and funny.

She had a plan to seduce him once he'd finished his call. So far this week he hadn't touched her other than to guide her into a room with his hand on her back. Ingrid assumed that he wanted a full-service week, but so far they had talked, eaten excellent food prepared by the house keeper, and had visited the beautiful Sussex coastline.

Removing her red lace thong, she draped it over her unused wine glass. Lifting her long, lean legs, toned from her daily run, she rested the heels of her red stilettos on the tablecloth, either side of her empty plate. The crisp white wine had yet to be poured, the condensation dripped down the outside of the bottle. The angle of her legs caused the hem of her short, flared, red dress to drop to her thighs. She hoped his eyes were drawn to her exposed skin as he walked out onto the balcony. She couldn't see another soul, just the ocean as it crashed against the rocks on the peninsula.

Ingrid dropped her head back and draped her arms over the chair's arms as the sun warmed her face.

"You look beautiful draped over the lunch table, good enough to eat," Harvey said as he approached the veranda door. Undoing his tie, he pulled it off his neck, unbuttoned the top button of his shirt and came around the back of her chair. He took her right wrist and then her left and pulled them back behind her. She clasped her fingers together, and Harvey tied the silk tie around her wrists tightly.

"Is this okay?" He asked.

Ingrid sighed at his question, always a gentleman.

"Yes, this is okay," she answered and peered over her shoulder to catch his eye.

"You're the most gorgeous woman I have ever met," he said.

"Then what are you waiting for?" Ingrid asked.

"All in good time, sweetheart. My business dealings are over for the day, and now I want to enjoy your delicious body."

Harvey gathered up her long blonde hair with his fingers, he expertly looped the locks into a top knot and used a hair tie to secure Ingrid's hair on top of her head.

Ingrid kept quiet and let him do what he wanted. Harvey massaged her shoulders, pulling the spaghetti straps of her dress down her arms. The tops of her breasts were revealed, the round, full breasts, cupped in red lace heaving up and down with her anticipation. His hands stroked up her neck and then back down to her chest and into the cups of her bra. When he squeezed hard, Ingrid's head fell back against his taut stomach. Harvey pulled his hands away to undo the zip at the side of the dress. As the zip lowered, the dress loosened on her body and fell to her waist.

"Lift your hips, Ingrid," Harvey said, and when she did, he slipped the dress over her hips. Ingrid raised her knees and feet together so that Harvey could pull it off her body.

"Magnificent," Harvey said and leaned over Ingrid's shoulder and pulled her head back. Dropping his head, he kissed her roughly, firmly and with the passion of a man who knew his way around a woman's body. He stretched her mouth wide, dipping his tongue between her lips, but avoided toying with her tongue and closing his mouth over hers. One of his hands snaked down her body and between her legs. The glassware on the table clinked as she moved her heels to place them on the floor. Ingrid could feel the moisture pooling, completely turned on by Harvey's domination. He played with her clit, circling and pressing the flesh. Ingrid hummed her approval, hearing the sound of Harvey's fingers, sliding up and down her wet pussy. Her heavy breathing mixed in with Harvey's approval moans as he pushed his fingers inside her body caused Ingrid to part her legs further. She wanted him to fuck her hard, desperate for his cock to thrust inside her body. She didn't care whether it was her mouth, pussy, or ass. His fingers were pushing her towards an orgasm, but she needed more friction, to be stretched and feel the tip of his head hit her deep inside. She wanted the weight of his body on hers. Most of all, she wanted to touch him, but her hands were securely fastened behind her.

Harvey removed his hand from between her thighs, licking his fingers as he circled her chair. He pulled her chair to the side, away from the table. Dropping to his knees, smoothing his hands up her thighs Harvey took a deep breath and concentrated on where his hands were going. Using his thumbs, he parted her pussy lips and admired her, displayed in all her glory.

"Beautiful," he whispered.

Ducking his head down, he latched his mouth over her clit, sucking and biting the sensitive flesh. Swirling the tip of his tongue around her clit, he held her firmly in place with his hands on her thighs. Ingrid wanted to press her thighs tight against his head, but he kept her legs parted as far as she would let him. Licking and sucking, he carried on his assault, occasionally dipping his tongue into her wet core. Each time Harvey pressed his tongue hard to any part of her pussy, Ingrid whimpered. When her thighs started to quiver, Harvey pushed in two fingers as he flicked her clit with the tip of his tongue. He enjoyed the squirm of her hips to raise her pussy to his mouth. She tasted exquisite. His infrequent flicks sent Ingrid crazy with desire, her moans grew louder as she neared her orgasm. Just as she raised her heels to lift her knees, Harvey pulled away. Blowing cold air over Ingrid's exposed pussy lips, she cried out in anguish. Ingrid glared at Harvey as he stood in one fluid movement. His satisfied smirk irritated Ingrid to the point that she growled.

"You're magnificent, Ingrid. You'll get your orgasm when I get mine. We're going to come together. It's something I've always wanted but never achieved. I hope you don't mind waiting?" He asked.

Ingrid looked to Harvey, who now stood in between her legs, playing with her erect nipples through the lace. He squeezed and pinched hard. Ingrid couldn't believe his confession, why had he never come at the same time as his women did. She suspected she would never know.

"I can wait, I could murder you right now, but I'll wait. It's what you're paying for, after all," Ingrid said. She would do whatever it took to come at the same time as Harvey, there was no better feeling than reaching an orgasmic high together. Ingrid missed the wince that Harvey pulled at her words, he felt more than she did, but he wouldn't give up his game of seducing her. Three days he had talked to her to get to know her better and for him to reveal himself to see if she liked the man more than the money.

Harvey untied her wrists and massaged them back to life. Her fingertips had cooled, but not to the point that he'd cut off her circulation. He helped her stand and led her to their bedroom. He asked her to lie on the bed. He undressed and stood at the foot, gazing at her beautiful body. Taking his erection in hand, Harvey slowly stroked his hard cock. It was one thing to masturbate in the shower thinking of his fantasy girl, but a whole other experience to have a beautiful woman in his bed waiting to be fucked. He muttered a curse under his breath that he wasn't accomplished at seducing a woman who wasn't interested in his money. Hiring a high-end escort to satisfy his needs was a crazy thought he had a while back. He'd married twice, both women were matched with him by his mother for society's sake. He was nowhere near royalty status, but coming from old money meant that he had to marry high society women. Those women turned out to be cold vultures who didn't care about anything further than public appearances.

After his second marriage had failed, he swore that he wouldn't marry again. There were some nights where he encountered a woman who wanted one night of passion just as much as he did. The problem, was that they stuck to what they said, and left in the morning. He wanted to love a woman who would love, support, and cherish him, who had no other agenda than to share a life together. His first wife wanted a younger man to boss about. His second wife wanted him home by five every night. He couldn't run his business during the hours of nine to five. Each marriage lasted a year.

Harvey had handpicked Ingrid. He was under no illusion that he was paying her to be in his house and to do exactly as he asked, but Harvey told himself that she wanted to be there with him. When he'd received the phone call from Ingrid's Madam that she'd agreed on the spot, with no hesitation, he ignored the nagging thought that she saw him as a source of income. When Harvey picked Ingrid up from her home, he was surprised at the size of her house and where she'd lived. He wanted to believe that she didn't care about the money.

They had a connection, he could feel it.

Harvey had recently celebrated his forty-fifth birthday but still felt like a thirty-year-old. His boxing sessions kept him fit, the telltale sign that he was older than the average man at the gym was his grey hair. Harvey kept his salt and pepper hair cropped short at his nape but was long at the front. Thinking about his hair, he pulled his fingers through and sighed as he kept stroking his cock. Ingrid crossed her legs at her ankles and raised her arms above her head. The rise of her breasts, excited Harvey, the soft skin on the underside of her breasts was not visible. She smiled warmly and beckoned him to bed, parting her legs in invitation. Harvey let go of his cock and crawled up the bed, burying his face in the crook of her thigh kissing and sucking the sensitive skin next to her pussy lips. Ingrid squeezed her eyes shut, the frustration building once more in her belly. Harvey spread her pussy lips and licked slowly over her clit. Ingrid's breathing slowed to the same speed she rotated her hips. Harvey kept his rhythm with her movement, he needed her to be right on the edge of an orgasm. She dropped one hand to stroke his hair, clutching onto the long parts when she started to shake from his languid licks and bites.

He kissed her flat belly and in the valley between her breasts, he made his way up to her mouth and kissed her passionately while he positioned his body over hers. With his erection, he placed his hard cock where he wanted to slide into her body. The crown of his cock penetrated her warm core, and he nearly came at that moment. Hooking her leg over his forearm, he pushed her knee to her chest and nudged into her pussy an inch at a time. Harvey captured Ingrid's mouth with his, kissing her while he thrust inside until his balls hit her arse. Hooking her other leg up too, Harvey lifted his body off hers like he was set for press-ups. Now he was ready to work hard for his simultaneous orgasm.

"I'm ready Harvey, I'm going to come," Ingrid said in between her pants and moans. She slipped a hand between their bodies to stroke her clit.

"Come now, Ingrid, I need you to come right now," he yelled.

She furiously rubbed her clit in circles and raised her hips to meet his frantic thrusts. She felt him push all the way inside her, as far as her body would let him and clamped around his cock in spasms that crippled her. Ingrid cried out as the intense pulses rippled down over his cock. He held her in a chaste kiss as he stroked in and out of her body to keep the vibrations going for a few moments more.

"Fuck," he whispered as he pulled out of Ingrid's body and lay panting on his back next to her. "That was fucking awesome."

Ingrid couldn't answer, her heart beat frantically in her chest as she still felt the aftershocks of her orgasm. She gently played with her clit, a second orgasm was on the edge.

"Let me," Harvey said and took over softly playing with her swollen clit. He used his other hand to slip a thumb inside her core. Ingrid hid her face behind her hands and whimpered as her second orgasm arrived at a slower speed. This time a flash of heat spread over her body and the lazy shocks grabbed at Harvey's thumb.

Harvey pulled away and grabbed the duvet to cover up and around their bodies. He pulled her closer until they were nose to nose.

"I think we're going to get along just fine this week," he said and kissed her mouth.

Chapter 5

The following morning, Harvey returned to his work, and Ingrid wasn't surprised. A man like him couldn't give up working even for a couple of hours.

Flipping open her laptop, she stared at the ominous folder labelled *book*. Writing had never been her forte before she started writing for the column at *Ipris* and that come by accident. One Sunday morning, a few years ago, Ingrid had left a client as the skies were turning pink. Her stomach rumbled in protest of entertaining all night long. She knew of a deli bar that opened at 4am to sell its freshly baked bread to the surrounding cafes. She'd known the owner of the shop for years. Tucked away in a quiet street of London, was the baby blue painted cafe. Chairs that reminded her of her school days scraped across the floor as she entered. A few late night revellers were just leaving. In the far corner by the stack of the day's newspapers, was a striking brunette hunched over her laptop keyboard. The woman blindly reached for her coffee cup, took a sip and then placed it back perfectly on the saucer. Ingrid kept half an eye on the woman while she walked to the counter. Alan, the owner, greeted her with a warm hug and a brotherly kiss on the cheek.

"You're looking good, Ingrid, want some coffee?" Alan asked. He wiped off the flour from his hands on his apron and started banging the coffee machine part that needed fresh grounds.

Ingrid nodded. Looking over her shoulder and then to Alan. "Who's that?" She asked.

"She's something to do with a fashion magazine, one of the top ones. She comes in here as often as you do. I swear she has caffeine for blood." Alan said, laughing at his own joke.

When the latte was ready, Ingrid paid and took the table next to the woman. It was only after Ingrid had ordered a second coffee that the woman looked up from her screen. Turning her head to Ingrid, she smiled. It was one of those expressions when you instantly know you are sitting next to a kindred spirit. Ingrid introduced herself and found that within half an hour she had confessed what she did for a living. Her timing couldn't have been better, the woman, Rebecca Patterson was looking for a columnist to write about empowering women. Ingrid was doubtful at first, thinking that many would see having dates for money was the opposite of empowerment. Rebecca saw it as a conscious decision to do whatever she wanted and to hell with what people thought about it.

Their friendship was three years old, and that's how long she had been writing for *Ipris*. She had hundreds of stories written, most of them didn't make it to the magazine. They were too risque for the boss to handle in his magazine. Those were turned down, but she still had a wealth of stories that Rebecca could choose from. Rebecca had told her after a year that Harvey Hinder read each story before it was published. Ingrid wasn't entirely convinced that she was his date this week by chance, or that her Madam had given her this client as a final goodbye.

A text message on her phone diverted her thoughts. Picking up her phone, she read the preview and then unlocked the screen.

Lucas: I'm in trouble

The first time Ingrid had met Lucas was at a party for a client. It wasn't usual for the escorts to meet each other. Her Madam didn't like it, most of the time neither did the escorts. Their preference was to be anonymous in the world of forbidden and sordid sex. The client had asked for two people, one man and one woman of differing ages. Lucas and Ingrid fit the criteria. They had formed a loose friendship after that, never meeting but were always in contact by phone. It mainly consisted of Lucas calling her to work through his problems.

"What's wrong?" Ingrid said, not bothering with any greeting when he picked up her call after one ring.

"I've fallen for a client," Lucas said.

Ingrid could hear the exhale of smoke once he'd finished talking. He only ever smoked when he was under immense pressure to look waif-like for the catwalks of Milan and Paris. If Lucas couldn't eat, then he'd smoke, or fuck. Fucking was few and far between for Lucas, he had to take the jobs at short notice when he knew he wasn't needed for a fashion appointment. Being a top male model was his passion, but he wanted to buy his first home with cash. Ingrid understood the aversion to having any debt and didn't comment on his plans. She preferred not to know what drove an escort to do what they did. Her reasons were entirely her own, and she wouldn't share them with anyone, they were no one else's business.

"You idiot, who is she?"

"Her name's Ursula, and she is the sweetest, filthiest woman I have ever met. She's the one for me. The problem is, I met her as an escort. We had the best sex I've ever had, I just don't know what to do next," Lucas said.

The silence filled the telephone line, Ingrid keeping quiet to let Lucas talk more but nothing was coming from him.

"I'll figure it out, thanks for listening," Lucas said and ended the call.

"Before you go, I have good news and bad news. The good news is that Rebecca wants you as the new writer for *Ipris*, she'll get in contact with you soon."

"And the bad news?" He asked.

"You need to find another date for Saturday," Ingrid said.

"Ok, no problem, I might take this girl, if she'll have me," he said.

Ingrid took the phone from her ear and stared at the screen to see if he was still there. He'd hung up. She tapped out a quick message for him to call her if he needed to and set it aside.

"Who was that?" Harvey said from the doorway.

"A friend. The fool's fallen in love," Ingrid said. She tapped a few keys on the keyboard and then closed the lid.

"Love is the most amazing feeling in the world. It's one of the few things you don't have any control over. Don't you think?"

"I've never been in love, I wouldn't know," she said. Her empty words echoed around the dining room.

"Never?" Harvey asked, incredulousness coming through as he spoke.

"No, never," Ingrid said.

Harvey had joined her at the dining table, pushing the laptop out of reach. He took her hand in his, stroking her palm with his thumb. "I've never liked anyone long enough to fall in love. It's why I enjoy this job so much, no attachments. Perfect really."

"Then why are you giving it all up?"

"What makes you think I'm giving up my job?"

"Your Madam told me," Harvey said and kept her hand firmly in his. "We have known each other a long time, I don't think she meant to say, she probably didn't realise she wasn't supposed to."

Ingrid remained quiet, thinking about the too many coincidences. She was due to meet Tessa Wilby in half an hour and didn't have time to quiz Harvey about what he knew about her. It was a possibility that he knew Ingrid wrote for the magazine. If that were true, she would wait for him to tell her.

"She doesn't generally tell anybody anything, let alone what my future intentions are," Ingrid said.

Harvey shifted in his seat and let her hand drop to the table, he covered her hand, massaging her fingers. Ingrid noted what he was doing and relaxed. A slice of guilt ran through her that she was his anonymous writer, a compulsion to confess overcame her.

"Maybe she was having an off day. Anyway, I'm curious," he said.

Coming around the back of her chair, he stroked her neck with the back of his hand. She dropped her head and took a deep breath. His touch was gentle, reverent, she was beginning to enjoy his touch. This was new to her, but then spending five days with a man was new to her, it was usually a one night deal.

"What are you curious about?" She asked, her voice barely above a whisper.

"What you will do next."

"I'm going to write a book," she said.

Sidestepping out of the chair and away from the glass dining room table, her mind wandered. Later, she hoped Harvey would lay her on the glass after dinner and indulge in oral sex.

"Do you have a publisher interested?"

"No, I haven't got that far. I've got to go, Harvey, I'm running late,"

"I thought I had you exclusively this week," Harvey said. It was the first time he had shown any annoyance.

He came to stand at her side, holding her hand in one and lifting her chin with the other. He held her gaze, waiting for an answer. His eyes showed pain with the thought that she might be spending time with another man. Ingrid waited a moment to answer, why did he care if she had another client at the same time. They had safe sex, he knew what she did for a living, why would he have an issue with it, she wondered.

"It's not a date. I'm meeting with an editor. I told you about my appointments in the car on the way down here," she said. She didn't mean to sound irritated, but she was used to rules, and the fact that he was questioning her meant that this wasn't a rule driven job.

Kissing his cheek, she pulled away only to be pulled back to his chest. Harvey wrapped his arms around her back and kissed her mouth, gently pushing his tongue into her open mouth. They grew heated in their passion, he pushed her up against the table and Ingrid manoeuvred her bottom to sit on the glass.

Pulling Harvey between her legs by his tie, she pulled his shirt out of his trousers.

"We have to be quick, I don't want to make a wrong impression with Tessa," Ingrid said between her kisses.

"Tessa Wilby?" Harvey asked.

He opened the large buttons at the front of Ingrid's denim dress until it fell open. The baby blue bra and knickers set highlighted Ingrid's tanned body.

"The very same, do you know her?" Ingrid asked already knowing that Tessa worked for one of his magazines. She didn't expect him to know that, he must have thousands working for him.

"She works for me," he said.

Harvey surprised her with his knowledge of his staff. She ignored the mounting coincidences. Of all the editors he knew on his payroll, it was the same editor that she worked with.

Ingrid groaned when his hands pulled her knickers off. He unzipped his trousers, leaving his belt done up. Sheathing his cock, once he'd freed his erection, he grinned at Ingrid and pulled her to the edge of the table. Thrusting inside her, Harvey rested his head on her shoulder, his palms flat on the glass. Ingrid tilted her hips and lifted her legs to wrap around his waist. Rubbing her clit as he pumped in and out of her pussy had her calling out her orgasm in minutes. Harvey soon followed and bit her shoulder gently to hide the roar he wanted to let out. He would never grow tired of simultaneous orgasms with Ingrid, or almost simultaneous in this case. He'd never enjoyed an orgasm within the same five minutes of any woman he had fucked. Pulling away, he discarded the condom and redressed. Ingrid had to find her knickers before she could be presentable to meet Tessa. Harvey had kept them in his trouser pocket, handing them over after a few minutes of Ingrid searching for them.

"I was tempted to let you leave without these," he said and had her underwear dangling from his finger. She turned and glared at him for a moment.

Harvey crouched and held out her knickers for her to step into. He stood as he pulled the satin underwear up her legs and in place. He gently rubbed through the silky material, over her clit and relished the throaty moan Ingrid let out.

"Hurry back, and say hello to Tessa for me," Harvey said and kissed Ingrid before he left the dining area of the living room.

Ingrid, confused for a moment, took in what had happened in the last ten minutes. She'd enjoyed a client's touch, confessed what her plans were, and thought that she wanted to hurry back for him. Calling Lucas a fool earlier may be Karma's way of reminding her that attraction to a client can happen to the unlikeliest of people. Her distant attraction to this man before they'd met had solidified in record time.

She grabbed her bag and left the house to get to her appointment with Tessa.

Chapter 6

Ingrid didn't know Jackson's Bay or where the cafe was situated that Tessa had suggested they meet at, ten minutes ago. She stood on the doorstep of the mansion and looked down the long driveway. It would take her a while to walk into town, Ingrid wondered if Harvey would give her a lift. They had a deal when she took the job that she could come and go as she pleased. Harvey had stipulated that she needed to spend every evening and night with him, but the daytime they could improvise.

She didn't know what his plans were today, she hadn't asked and guilt laced through her once again. He'd seemed disappointed that she was leaving him for the afternoon.

"Do you need a lift?" Harvey asked, hoola hooping set of car keys around his finger.

Ingrid turned around to see that Harvey had changed clothes into jeans and a t-shirt. His handsome face was hopeful.

"Yes, I do, if it doesn't cause you any problems," Ingrid said.

"I can drop you where you need to be. I don't usually venture into town. I'm the mysterious ogre according to the young adults around here."

Ingrid followed Harvey around the side of the mansion and to the garage. They entered the spacious garage, where several cars were lined up in a row. Each vehicle a different type and style. Ingrid had shoes for all occasions, it seemed that Harvey had a car for all occasions. When he pressed the key fob, a beautiful navy sports car flashed its indicators. With another press of a button, the roof came down.

"Why are you an ogre?"

"Behind the house is a lake, it's a man-made one that my grandfather had built before I was born. It was for my father and his brothers and sisters to play in. He was obsessed with security and didn't trust any of them to be safe going to the local beach. My brothers and I played in that lake, but none of us have children, so it goes unused. Kids sneak in, kissing and groping on the shoreline and some of them skinny dip. I don't want to look out my bedroom window and see kids making out by my lake. I tend to lean out the window, yell at them and then let off a flare."

Ingrid laughed, holding her stomach.

"For someone who is in love with the idea of love you have a funny way of showing it," Ingrid said, trying to get her giggles under control.

Harvey accelerated out of the garage and down the driveway. She hadn't noticed that he was wearing brown leather gloves until that moment. He held the gear stick with authority, and it inexplicably turned her on. She had a vision of those gloved hands holding a crop while she was lay spreadeagled on the dining room table.

"You stopped laughing, what are you thinking about?" Harvey asked.

He turned onto the side road and headed to the cafe Ingrid had mentioned before they set off.

"Nothing, I was noticing your gloves, I like them," Ingrid said.

Harvey smiled and looked in his rear view mirror. Taking his hand off the gear stick, and onto Ingrid's thigh, he stroked her leg once and then put his hand on the steering wheel.

"Maybe I'll wear these gloves later."

Ingrid grinned. She put on her sunglasses and watched as the houses passed by. They were soon in the centre of the town at a set of traffic lights. Harvey pointed to the cafe she needed, and when the lights turned green, he moved forward slowly and parked up on the side of the road.

"Kiss me goodbye," Harvey said.

He held onto the steering wheel with one hand and pulled her gently toward him, hooking one finger into the cleavage of her dress. Ingrid kissed him sweetly before exiting the car.

"I'll see you later, and leave the loved-up kids alone," Ingrid said and smiled when he rolled his eyes.

"Give me a call when you're done, I'll come and pick you up. We can get an early dinner at a pub I like a few miles away."

"Okay," she agreed and gave him a shy smile. As each hour passed, she acted more like a girlfriend in a new relationship than an experienced escort.

Chapter 7

Ingrid hopped out of the car, far more pleased than she should be that she liked her client. She heard his car pull away from the parking space and roar down the road. The cafe's red metal chairs glinted on the summer's day. Grateful for the light denim short dress keeping her cool in the heat of the morning, she shouldered her handbag and headed indoors into the shade. Tessa Wilby's wild red curly hair drew Ingrid to the back table like a beacon.

Ingrid placed a hand on Tessa's bare shoulder to alert her. Tessa stood immediately and hugged her friend.

"Hey, babe, you look fantastic. Your eyes are bright and full of mischief, have you been writing this morning?" Tessa asked and nodded to the barista behind the counter. Tessa had already given Ingrid's order when she arrived but told him to hold off making the Americano until her friend arrived.

"No writing so far today. This morning was about the real thing," Ingrid said, smirking at Tessa's wide eyes.

"I thought you were giving up your job?"

Ingrid hesitated to tell Tessa that her client was Harvey, even though he had asked her to say hello on his behalf. The problem was that Harvey didn't know that Tessa knew she was an escort. The warring decisions fought in her head. Her instinct was to protect Harvey's reputation. If he wanted her to say hello on his behalf, then he wanted Tessa to know he was dating her. Ingrid's mind fell apart for a moment. She didn't know what was going on.

"This is my last client, my Madam asked me to take on one more job as a favour. He's a great guy, which is a bonus in my line of work. He's asked me to go to the *Ipris* Gala," Ingrid said.

"I don't have a date for the gala or a dress. That means I don't have shoes or a bag, maybe I shouldn't go," Tessa said, chewing her thumbnails.

"You won't have any nails left either if you keep biting them. Do you want me to find you a date, honey?" Ingrid said, knowing full well what the answer would be.

"Good God, no, I couldn't cope with that kind of date," Tessa said. She sat fully straight in her chair. "I love sex but struggle to express what I want. Each time I'm in bed with a hot man, I take my guidance from the man, often leaving the next morning unfulfilled. Taking an escort as a date and then ending up in bed with him would be too much pressure to perform. I want a man who desires me, just as I am."

"Sounds like you need a night of wild sex with no strings. Let me set you up. You know you'll have fun. It'll be on the house, a gift from me to say thank you for helping me with my book."

"You pay me plenty for my help, I don't want any more of your generosity. I'll find a date." Tessa said not believing a word of it.

"You know I can fix you up at a moment's notice so please call me if you need to. There's nothing wrong with going solo either, you could take your pick of the single handsome men. All those smoking hot bodies in tuxedo suits."

"You are a terrible influence, but I like it," Tessa said and laughed. "Let's get down to business so I can stuff my face with this Eccles cake," Tessa said pointing to the plate next to her empty coffee mug.

Ingrid's coffee had arrived, along with a coconut macaroon. Ingrid drank and ate while Tessa talked about the draft copy of the book Ingrid had mapped out, explaining the process and what needed to happen next. Ingrid stared at Tessa opened mouthed when she was told that three publishing houses wanted to sign a contract with her. The volume of work could easily stretch to five books. Ingrid had a bidding war over the rights to the stories.

"Well, fuck, what the hell should I do?" Ingrid said.

"You'll have to answer that question. Meet with them all and see who you get on with the best, but also who is going to look after your interests. You want to remain anonymous, so push that point and see who breaks and who stands firm. You'll have a new editor, so you'll lose me, I'm sorry to say."

Ingrid stared again, this time her eyebrows furrowing. Ingrid trusted Tessa, she understood her point of view without judgement. She didn't want to start again with another editor and have to argue about what she did and didn't want to write.

"That's the deal breaker, we come as a package, we'll write these books together. I'll insist and see who takes me up on offer. That will be the publishing house that gets the stories." Ingrid huffed and dropped her hands into her lap, staring straight at Tessa, daring her to disagree. Tessa's small smile turned into a grin, nodding more vigorously as she thought it through.

"That could work, that could definitely work," Tessa said.

They stood and hugged to seal the deal. Ingrid's heart beat fast as she thought about the future, no longer scared that she was leaving the comfort of her decade-long career as an escort. She told her goodbyes to Tessa, promising to catch up with her at the gala and dialled Harvey's number.

Harvey arrived outside the cafe a few minutes later, wearing the sexiest smile she'd ever seen.

"Were you waiting for me?" Ingrid asked as she sat in the passenger seat.

"Maybe. I needed to do a few things in town. I hung around. Where's my kiss?" Harvey asked.

He held onto the steering wheel to reach across to Ingrid. He kissed her sweetly on the lips and then pulled out into the traffic. Ingrid struggled with the comfort she was feeling being in the company of Harvey. The thought of getting back to his home and undressed, had her shifting in her seat. The thought of Harvey's large, strong hands on her breasts caused her cheeks to flush. She hoped her oversized aviators covered any hint that she was looking forward to fucking him again.

"How was your meeting?" Harvey asked.

"Ridiculous," Ingrid said, glad for the change of subject in her head of Harvey fucking her.

"I'll fire her immediately," Harvey said.

They'd stopped at a set of traffic lights, and it took a moment for Ingrid to understand what he'd said. She turned in her seat and slipped off her glasses. Harvey's profile was mouth watering. His jaw line and high cheek bones were so defined she thought they were the work of a plastic surgeon. When he turned to look at her, his frown lines indicated that he'd never gone under the knife and was naturally handsome.

"Don't fire Tessa, I adore her. It's not her that is ridiculous, it's what she said that has blown my mind."

Ingrid faced the windscreen, admiring the view as they drove along the coast road.

"You can't clam up now, tell me what happened. I can't fix what I don't know," Harvey said.

"There's nothing to fix. Three publishing houses are competing for my work. I can take my pick, and that is staggering."

"Of course they are, you're a brilliant writer," Harvey said.

His smile depicted pain. No teeth were showing in his grimace and Ingrid was on high alert.

"How would you know, Harvey?" She asked, carefully.

Harvey pulled over on the side of the road near his house. He switched off the engine and tapped his closed fist on the steering wheel lightly.

"Confession time?" He asked.

Ingrid nodded.

"I know who you are, I know that you write for *Ipris*. I've read every one of your stories. It was me who decided which ones would be published and which ones didn't make the cut."

Ingrid's eyebrows rose above her aviators, and Harvey held up his hands.

"Not because they weren't any good, but some of them gave too much away about who you are. I didn't want to share too much of you. It killed me to know you were going on all these dates and none of the men were me. There were a few parties I saw you at and had to leave after ten minutes because I couldn't stand to watch you laugh and talk to anyone but me."

Harvey stopped talking, waiting for Ingrid to speak. Her head was bowed, but he could almost hear the cogs whirring in her mind.

"So, we've both been admiring each other from afar?" Ingrid said.

"You admire me?" Harvey said, astonished that she knew anything about him to admire. He pulled off her glasses and lifted her chin. He wanted to see the truth in her eyes.

"You're a brilliant man and to steal the phrase from my Madam, you're hot as fuck," Ingrid said. "Why did you wait so long to approach me?"

"I thought I had time, I figured I had all the time in the world. It didn't occur to me that you would give up the escort life. I was scared that if you weren't an escort, you wouldn't agree to go on a date with me. And that's where it gets messed up because I want you to like me for me and not for my money. I've paid your Madam an enormous amount of money to get you to have one last job."

Harvey let out an anguished, frustrated cry, turning away and getting out of the car. He strode over to the stone wall that acted as the entrance to his home and planted the palms of his hands on the cold stone wall. Dropping his head, he shook it from side to side to shake the fucked up methods he'd used to get to know Ingrid better, from his mind. He was about to tell her to forget the week, and she could leave, when her hands landed on his sides. She smoothed up to his shoulder blades and then scooted around, so her back was flat against the wall.

"I didn't think you would give me the time of day because I was an escort. I thought you would be disgusted about my job. When my Madam called me to say that you wanted to spend a week with me, I had to deliberately hold off blurting yes for a few minutes in an act of professionalism."

Harvey cupped her cheeks, gazed at her eyes, seeking the truth. When he decided that she was as genuine as he hoped she was, he kissed her. A soft, beseeching kiss, pleading with her to give him a chance.

"Are you here because of the money or because you want to be here with me?" Harvey asked.

"If it makes you feel any better, I'll donate your fee to charity. I'm here because I want to be, I'm here because I wanted to get to know you better to see if what I've admired for years is the real deal."

Harvey kissed her again, taking a mental note to match her donation to charity.

"Let's go inside, there must be a hard surface we haven't christened yet," Harvey said and hauled her back to the car before speeding down the driveway.

Chapter 8

Harvey lounged on the sofa, reading the morning paper, dismissing the idea of working. He'd had another epic night of sex with Ingrid. He'd abandoned the idea of going out for dinner and instead cooked them a late supper. Ingrid had talked about her plans to write a book of her memoirs, refusing his offer to help in choosing a publisher. They'd agreed to spend the day apart. Harvey hadn't expected to enjoy Ingrid's company as much as he did. Her humour and sass made him laugh until he felt it in his belly. Reluctantly leaving the bed this morning, Harvey took a look at the long legged beauty wrapped up in the bed sheets. Her flawless skin enticed him to touch and explore, but he knew if he caressed her smooth legs, he would end up fucking her awake.

Harvey had an hour until he was meeting his younger brother, Ramsay. It had been too long since they last met up. They were close, speaking regularly on the phone but their work schedules never got them in the same place at the same time very often. The *Ipris* Gala event was the only time guaranteed that they would see each other to catch up. Ramsay had been at the smaller charity soiree the previous night, and Harvey wasn't holding up much hope that he wouldn't be worse for wear.

Taking Ingrid into town to meet with her editor was perfect timing. With a bit of luck, when she finished, he'd be waiting to take her home after he met with Ramsay. The heat of the morning wrapped around him like a duvet on a winter's night. He couldn't remember the last time Jackson's Bay had suffered from a heat wave.

He usually parked in a private garage he owned in the back streets of the town. Harvey didn't like to leave his car in the open car park or the street. Spending tens of thousands of pounds on a car only to have idiots scratch the sides caused him unnecessary grief. The proportionate response to a damaged car would be to get it repaired, but once it was damaged, he no longer wanted to drive the vehicle. He wanted perfection in his motor vehicles. Harvey loved to drive beautiful cars so having a garage in town made sense to him. He didn't care that his brother ripped the piss out of him for it.

As Harvey pulled up to the red brick building, he pressed a button on the remote near the gear stick and watched the grey shutter doors arch up and back. Clutching onto the steering wheel, Harvey hit the brakes moments after he started to move forward. There in front of him was his brother, leaning casually against the brick wall, twirling a set of keys. Reversing back and then moving forward to park next to Ramsay's car, he slammed the car door when he got out.

"You scared the god damn shit out of me, I just lost five years of my life," Harvey said, well natured as he approached his brother for a hug.

They slapped each other's backs as they held firm for a moment and then broke apart.

"How are you little brother, you're looking younger and younger while I age away before my very eyes," Harvey said.

"Don't be ridiculous, you look younger than me," Ramsay said.

Any onlooker would have placed them at the same age. They both took care of their bodies, spending time at the gym and resting when they could. They'd seen their dad work himself into an early grave in his mid-sixties. They vowed they would not do the same.

"Let's go and get a coffee, I might treat myself to a Chelsea Bun too," Harvey said as he led the way from the garages and onto the high street. They took a left until they reached the pedestrianised road that housed all the cafes and small restaurants. All the shops had outside areas, some had invested in the last week with chairs and tables, making the most of the heat wave. Harvey knew which cafe he wanted, he had been visiting the blue fronted, single storey building most of his life. It was run by the same family he knew as a kid. Back then, he would go for an ice cream when his parents were out of town, and he was taken care of by his nanny. Ramsay was five years younger than him, so by the time Ramsay was asking for ice cream, Harvey was too busy with his mates to take him. A pang of guilt flashed through his heart for a moment.

"Shall we get an ice cream instead?" Harvey asked his brother.

They stood in front of the glass freezer looking at the array of different flavours.

"I'll have double mint choc chip with a flake," Ramsay said. "And a bottle of still water."

"Feeling hung-over?" Harvey asked with a chuckle. He gave his order to the girl behind the counter and rested his hip on the freezer.

"No, I only had one drink. I think I met the woman of my dreams. I have never seen a woman run so gracefully in heels as she did. She's funny, gorgeous, smart and did I mention she can run in heels? Her name's Jessica." Ramsay said.

"I need to meet this woman because you're a choosy fucker when it comes to women. When are you seeing her again?"

"Fuck off, you're choosier than I am," Ramsay said and took the ice cream from the girl.

Harvey paid for the ice creams and drinks while Ramsay took a seat at the nearest table.

"Well, I have a date this week, so I can't be that choosy, and she's a real firecracker," Harvey announced.

"Mine ended up pretending to be my wife at last night's party. Why weren't you there? I was expecting to see you," Ramsay said.

"I was busy. Mine is my pretend girlfriend, except I'm paying her," Harvey confessed and closed his eyes waiting for the condescending look his brother would inevitably give him.

"Are you ever going to trust a woman again with your heart? They're not all after your huge bank balance."

"*Our* huge bank balance," Harvey chastised. "I like this one. I've been following her progress for a while, I'm hoping that we can see each other, in a less formal arrangement. Apparently, she likes me too."

"You sound like a stalker. Explain before I go and warn this woman," Ramsay said, his friendly nudge let Ramsay know he was joking.

"She writes under a pen name for the magazine. She's the woman who writes the escort article every month. I read them before they go to print and have rejected a lot of the stories.

I feel protective of this woman, she seems to be wanting a life away from the escort industry. When I read her last story that said she was giving up, I called in a favour with her Madam to be her last client. Took some persuading, but she is in my bed for a week, and I have that time to seduce her."

Harvey's face looked relaxed as he spoke about the woman he had paid for. It was the first time in years that Ramsay had seen his brother laughing about a woman he was dating.

"She sounds like the perfect woman for you, good luck, brother. I need to figure out how I can get Jessica, the super model, to fall in love with me by Sunday morning. I have four days to make it work," Ramsay said.

"Are you talking about Jessica Dockery, the supermodel and feature editor of our magazine?" Harvey asked.

"It's your magazine. I don't have the first clue how to run our family empire. I'm perfectly happy designing shoes. Yes, she is the very same."

"Are you going to hand make her a pair of shoes? I remember when you used to make all of your own. The equipment is still at the house." Harvey reminded his brother.

"That's an excellent idea, I could bring her over tomorrow, and that could be a way to her heart. She said last night that she would sell her kidneys for a pair of handmade shoes."

Harvey raised his water bottle and waited for his brother to bump bottles.

"We may both end up with girlfriends we actually like by the time the week finishes. You just need to come up with a hair brained idea so I can woo Ingrid," Harvey said.

"If your Ingrid works for the magazine, Rebecca Patterson will know her. Nothing gets past that woman. She will know how you can seduce her," Ramsay offered.

They had moved away from the cafe and headed back to where the cars were safely parked.

"That's a good idea, thanks."

Each man reversed out of the garage and out onto the road, their unison horn blares startled a few passersby and then they were gone in different directions. Both on their way to find out how to seduce their women.

Chapter 9

Harvey had no idea how Ingrid was going to spend her day. They hadn't talked about her plans for Friday. He'd given her the privacy he would anyone he was dating. The suspicion that she may not leave her escort life and start booking more clients burned away at his heart, he rubbed the flat of his hand on his chest to rid the heartburn crawling its way up from his gut. Ingrid had promised him that she was only spending time with him, this week. Her reassuring words stopped the jealousy forming and spreading like a disease around his mind. His brother's suggestion of calling Rebecca entered his head. He warred with calling her. It would mean Harvey would have to confess that he knew who Ingrid was to the magazine. It was schoolyard tactics, but he was desperate enough to give it a try.

He spun in his office chair, in the study in a full circle. When he landed back facing his desk, he dialled Rebecca's number. She answered on the second ring.

"Hi Harvey," Rebecca said. Her heavy breathing on the line sounded frantic.

"Did I interrupt something, I can call back?" Harvey said.

"Don't be silly, I've just finished a swim. Is everything okay for Saturday?"

"Yes, of course, Saturday is all set, you're in charge," Harvey said.

He was curious why she leapt to that conclusion of all the things she would guess at why he was calling.

"Thanks. All the preparations are made, will I see you there?"

A silence followed, he needed to talk to her about something that wasn't business. He'd only ever discussed the magazine with her. Switching the phone to speaker, he swayed side to side on his chair, plucking up the courage to broach the subject of Ingrid.

"We need to meet, what are you doing in an hour?" Harvey asked.

"I can fit you into my busy schedule, Harvey, are we having a conference call?"

"I'm in town, and I know you know this. There is one agenda item, Ingrid," Harvey said.

He heard the heavy sigh on the end of the phone and gave Rebecca enough time to agree to the meeting.

"Where do you want to meet?" She asked.

"There's a pub on Winston Street, *The White Hare*. They leave their tables and benches out over night, I'll meet you there," Harvey said and hung up.

He didn't doubt that Rebecca would turn up, but he wasn't sure that he would gain any real insight about Ingrid.

Chapter 10

I ngrid licked at an ice lolly, catching the melting juices running down her hand with her tongue. She'd arrived at the allotted bench, waiting for Lucas to turn up. She'd never known him to be on time for anything, which was why she was sucking on a lolly like she was four years old.

"What you're doing is obscene," Lucas said when as he flopped onto the bench next to her.

"Hello, to you too. There's no decent way to eat an ice lolly if you have a filthy mind," Ingrid answered.

"You're eating an ice lolly before breakfast. There's nothing dirty about my thoughts apart from who sells lollies at this time of the morning?" Lucas asked. He didn't want her to answer, he was moody that the only time she would meet him was a stupid o'clock in the morning. The only reason he agreed was that he wasn't sleeping well thinking of his blonde bombshell.

She'd just tossed the wooden stick in the bin next to her when her phone buzzed.

Rebecca: Why am I on my way to a meeting with Harvey at eight in the fucking morning and his only agenda item is you?

Ingrid hit dial on Rebecca's number.

"What the fuck?" Ingrid hissed down the phone. "Why is he meeting you?"

"I don't know, all I know is, he knows you work for me and he wants to discuss you. How's it been going this week?"

Ingrid paused answering for a moment, glancing at Lucas who was drawing on his cigarette, seemingly oblivious to Ingrid's high pitched conversation.

"It's been amazing, I really like the guy. I think he likes me too."

"Maybe he wanted to know about you, to make it a romance. This is like being at school, trying to find out if my mate fancies your mate. He knows we're best friends. If he had an issue with you writing for the magazine, he would have stepped in a long time ago. This is personal. How much do you want me to tell him?"

"If it's romance related, you can tell him anything you like. If it's work, then act dumb."

"Can I tell him that you've never slept with a client?"

"If you think that's appropriate," Ingrid said.

"I believe that's your worst fear, that you'd get found out."

"True. I like Harvey, tell the man whatever he wants to know," Ingrid said.

"Okay, got it. I'm here at the pub, so I'll update you later," Rebecca said.

The line went dead.

"So, I'm not the only one who has fallen for a client. I'm not the only stupid fool sitting on this bench. How about we help each other out?" Lucas said.

Ingrid glanced at Lucas, catching his eye, as soon as she did, she burst out laughing.

"What a pair we make, let's start with you. I reckon yours will be easier to solve. You've only been in the business a year, it should be straight forward for you to date a regular girl. Me, on the other hand, is not quite so simple. I have dated some high profile people. Those people will know Harvey. If he wants to date me without the professional price tag, it's going to be difficult for him to introduce me to his world."

"You're right, let's start with me. Your situation is already giving me a headache." Lucas said, lighting the second cigarette since he'd arrived.

"When was the last time you saw Ursula?"

"The night she hired me. Unless I knock on her door, I have no other way of contacting Ursula." Lucas slumped on the seat, his legs stretched out and crossed at the ankles. His skinny fit jeans accentuated is slim legs. Ingrid watched with amusement as Lucas tried three times to lift the neck of his hoodie using his chin to get comfortable. After angrily stuffing his hands into the pouch at the front, he took a look at Ingrid. "Stop laughing, it's not funny."

"Okay, okay, let's get some perspective here. You met her once for a couple of hours, and now you're in love."

"I stayed all night," he said quietly.

"She didn't pay for all night unless she's supremely wealthy. I bet Madam was rubbing her hands with glee over that one."

"Ursula only paid for two hours. I spent the rest of the time with her for free. She tried to pay me, but I refused. I'm so confused."

"Do you know how she feels about you?"

"No. I just know how we are together. We clicked, I've never had that before with anyone. Apart from you. You and I clicked as friends, but the connection I experienced with Ursula felt like more. I didn't want to leave the next morning. She made me breakfast and then I left. We had that weird lingering few minutes at the front door when we said goodbye."

"How many times did you fuck her?"

"Just the once, the once she paid for. We talked the rest of the time. I kissed her goodbye, it was the best kiss of my life. I don't believe there is a one sided kiss. You can't have that kind of fake passion."

"Says the escort," Ingrid replied.

"You know what I mean? Don't you? Please tell me you know what I'm saying before I cart myself off to the asylum."

Lucas let out an anguished cry to rival the seagulls who had found half a sandwich on the beach in front of them. It was loud enough for them to stop scrabbling over the bits and look their way.

"You are going to have to knock on her front door and ask her out on a proper date. Bring her to the *Ipris* Gala."

Uncharacteristically, Lucas flung his arms around Ingrid. She held him tight. Their friendship grew solid overnight the first time they met. She felt protective of the flamboyant, brash model who fucked for his future. They stayed cuddled on the bench for a while, chatting about his plan to win her heart. Ingrid made a move to get up after they had formed their plan.

"Do you want me to come with you?"

"No offence but it would look like my mum is dropping me off for a date," Lucas said as he dodged the smack Ingrid was about to give his arm.

"Hey, I'm not that old," she said.

"No, but I look younger than I am," he said.

Ingrid kissed and hugged him goodbye and walked back to the main road. Anxious to get back to Harvey, she hailed a taxi and headed back to the mansion.

Ingrid heard Harvey leave their bed just after dawn and he hadn't returned. When Lucas's text came through, she'd showered and dressed with no sign of Harvey coming back to bed. Ingrid had walked into town to reach Lucas. It was a relief when Rebecca told her she was meeting Harvey, she'd worried that he'd realised that he was foolish to want to spend time with her.

When she entered the mansion, it dawned on her that there wasn't any security stopping her. Walking back through the main door, she stood on the top step and looked up to the archway above her head. In the far corner, she spotted what she was looking for. A camera. It was currently trained on her. She moved to the left and then to the right. It silently moved with her.

"Are you playing with my security team?" Harvey asked. He'd propped his tall, lean body against the closed half of the front doors, his hands in his pockets.

"I wondered why it was the door was unlocked, and I could come and go as I pleased. I hadn't seen you this morning. Usually, I arrive with you. Are there cameras everywhere?" Ingrid asked, her mind went straight to their quick fucking on the dining room table.

"No. Just on the entrances. Security is in the back of the house. They have their own entrance, the housekeeper keeps them well fed and watered."

Harvey pushed off the door frame and circled his arms around her back. Kissing her lips once, he leaned back, staring at her mouth and kissed her again, taking a long sweep of her bottom lip. Harvey licked his lips again, frowning for a moment, and then his eyes went wide.

"Lemon sorbet ice lolly from Benny's?" Harvey asked.

"How the hell do you know that?" Ingrid was astonished at his accuracy. Benny's was the only place open at the time she strolled through the paved area of town. She wanted to get to the bench on time to make sure she hadn't missed Lucas. Exploring the other streets would have to wait for another time.

"I've lived in this town for a very long time and have tried every lolly and ice cream he sells."

Harvey was proud of his skills which made Ingrid laugh. She kissed him again until all traces of her sticky evidence had disappeared. He led her into the house and out to the back garden. The outdoor pool twinkled in the sunshine. He brought her to the shaded part of the garden on the other side of the pool and under an oak tree. They sat on what looked like a park bench, Ingrid smoothed over the small silver plate in the centre of the seat.

'In memory of our beloved mother and father who spent many hours sitting here, hand in hand.'

"That's beautiful," Ingrid said and looked to Harvey. He was sitting at the other end of the seat with the plaque in between them.

Harvey's smile was rueful as he touched the words with the tip of his finger. Some of the ink had faded on the stamped letters, but she could still read the words clearly.

"They loved sitting out here on summer mornings and winter evenings. My brother and I would look here if we couldn't find them in the house. It was their affection and love for one another that made me fall in love with love."

Ingrid lost Harvey for a few minutes. She kept quiet assuming he was replaying a memory. His eyes glassed over as he leant back on the bench. He raised his arm and beckoned Ingrid to slide across and nestle at his side. The sun warmed their skin through the leaves of the great oak, and she sagged at his side.

"How's Rebecca?" Ingrid asked to break the intense silence.

Harvey paused and then chuckled.

"I should've known she'd call you. She's fine, she looks great actually. Taking time off suits her, I should insist she does that more often. She told me a secret, and I want to talk to you about it."

Ingrid stiffened at his side, she had no idea what Rebecca had said. Especially as they hadn't spoken after she'd met with Lucas. A thousand things ran through her head of all the stories Ingrid had handed over to Rebecca and searched her memory for anything that she would now be ashamed about. Then after speed reading her last ten years in her head, she realised that Harvey had also read those stories too. It left one thing. The no sex with clients part.

"What secret did she reveal?"

"You never sleep with your clients. You slept with me, I want to know what that means?"

"I'm attracted to you, I have been for a long time. You didn't touch me for two days, and it drove me crazy. I forgot that you were paying me to spend time with you."

Another stretch of silence followed, he held her tighter to his side. He kissed the top of her head and sighed.

"I want to take you to the *Ipris* Gala as my girlfriend," Harvey spoke with certainty, Ingrid couldn't detect the question only the statement.

"I don't think that's a good idea," Ingrid said and pulled out of his embrace, she straddled his lap so that she could look at him, talk some sense into him. "There is bound to be someone who has met me before, I don't want to embarrass you on the night of your gala. It's a huge celebration, and it's going to make headline news for all the right reasons."

"I don't care what they say," he said and grabbed her waist.

Ingrid laughed involuntarily as his fingers grabbed just under her ribs. Harvey narrowed his eyes as he made the same movement again. Ingrid started to laugh again and pointed her finger at him, pursing her lips.

"Don't Harvey," she warned.

"Are you ticklish, Ingrid?"

Ingrid moved to get off his lap, but he was too quick. He tickled her sides until she was laughing uncontrollably, squirming on his lap and his growing erection.

"I love your laughter, it's been too long since there has been happiness on this bench," Harvey said and kissed her lips.

Just as their kiss was getting heated, they heard a slamming of a door. Harvey's head whipped around to the small building on the side of the house.

"My brother's here, let's go meet him. I think he has a girl with him. He says that she is the woman for him. He's a choosy fucker so I can't wait to meet her."

Ingrid climbed off Harvey but didn't move from standing in front of him.

"Are we a thing?" Ingrid asked.

"A thing? Is that kid talk for girlfriend and boyfriend?"

"Yeah, are we?"

"Only if you come to the Gala with me as a date," Harvey said.

Ingrid didn't answer as she followed him to the outer stone building on the other side of the pool. She needed to give him an answer, but fear threaded itself through her heart and mind. Even if Harvey said he didn't care about her career choice, the first time someone called him out on it, he would care.

"This is my brother's workshop. He makes shoes. I'm so proud of him, he's done so well for himself with no help from me at all. Do you want to meet him?"

"Yes, introduce me to your brother," Ingrid said and nodded. She'd made her decision.

Jessica and Ramsay

Chapter 1

Jessica Dockery loved Jackson's Bay. She fell in love with the town five years ago when she'd attended her first *Ipris* Gala. Living in London was perfect for her modelling career in her early years, but there came a time when Jessica wanted peace and quiet to think and plan. Jackson's Bay was perfectly situated only half an hour from Gatwick airport, and an hour from London. She could still access her career and have her quiet time. She loved her quiet time more than anything else in the world. When Jessica went house hunting, she found her perfect house on the first day of searching. Her house, in the back streets of the town, was a tardis of a building. From the front, it looked pokey, bijou and tired, but she fell in love with it, anyway. After the front had been painted a striking yellow to contrast with the other terraced houses in the street, she got to work on the back garden. The front door opened directly on the street, but the garden at the back was one hundred feet of grass and nothing else. Jessica wanted the garden to be her haven.

Experts came in to get to work on her house while Jessica was away on the other side of the world, strutting down various catwalks. She added a large wooden shed at the end of the garden. The shed had a day bed, a writer's desk, and a fridge full of wine, the wifi reached that far too. Lanterns hung from the ceiling and she had heat in the winter. It was her escape from her model life, a place she could be alone with no one fussing with her hair or applying false eyelashes. When Jessica was at home, she didn't wear any makeup, it gave her skin time to breathe as well as her mind to zone out.

The rest of the garden was kept as grass. Jessica wasn't home long enough to take care of plants or flowers and didn't see the point in hiring a gardener to maintain the place that no one saw. Her decking outside the back door had a swing seat and a fire pit. On the odd occasion, she had guests, that was where they congregated, with blankets and overstuffed cushions.

Her schedule allowed her a week off to enjoy the build up to the party, her driver service had dropped her off late last night, and now she stretched out on the decking in her swim suit soaking up the sunshine.

Nadia Rampling arrived at the back door holding two ice-cream cones with two scoops of lemon sorbet balanced on top.

"Did you ever worry that you were the wrong shape? That you weren't fat enough to wear the plus size model cape and crown?" Nadia said as she padded barefoot onto the decking. She took the swing seat in the shade and nudged Jessica's foot.

Jessica shielded her eyes to look over at Nadia. Her mouth dropped open as she eyed the sorbet cone. Lemon was her favourite flavour, in fact, Jessica was drawn to any sharp citrus smell or taste.

"Good morning, and no, I didn't," Jessica answered. "Why are you asking?"

"There are no plus size male models. They're just men, who model, why is that?" Nadia asked.

She'd sprawled length ways on the swing seat, kicking off her mules to get comfortable. Her pale blue shorts showing off her tanned legs.

"This is a bit philosophical for a Wednesday, what or who have you been reading about?" Jessica said.

"I was trying to think who would be a good pairing for me on the *Ipris* cover next month and I couldn't think of a single plus size male model. Compared to most male and female models I am large. Even my mum thinks I'm fat."

"Men aren't objectified, not like women are. Their body shape and size is not a constant talking point where women's are. There is not an equivalent to feminism in the male world, they are just, men. Which means you don't get the arguments of a size 14 shirt collar size is the best collar size to be. It just doesn't happen. My mission in life is to get you to ignore what your mother tells you. You're not fat."

Nadia sat back up to finish her cone, the sorbet dripping down her hand and narrowly missing her loose cotton shirt. Jessica thought that Nadia worried too much about the model industry and told her daily to not get too hung up about what was said in the press. She also urged Nadia not to read the comments on her Instagram feed, but it fell on deaf ears.

"I'm worried about the cover of the anniversary issue. What if I'm twice the size of the model they put me with?"

"I know which model you are shooting the cover with and you are not twice his size. You've lurched from the wrong shape to too big in one conversation. What is going on?"

"Who is it? Is he handsome and muscular?"

"You'll see next week when you arrive at the shoot, now tell me what's really going on?"

"I had the best sex of my life last night. He didn't hesitate when he saw me naked. His eyes ate up the vision of my curves. I'd never had that before, I've never experienced a man have passionate sex with me and not care that my thighs jiggle," Nadia confessed. "Is that too much sharing, I'm sorry," Nadia said and smacked her forehead in embarrassment.

"Don't be ridiculous, you can share anything you like. It's been a bloody long time since a man looked at me that way let alone strip me and fuck me. Who is your new man?"

"His name's Finn, he's off to study graphic design at Uni in the autumn. He's here on holiday with his family from London, but plans to move here while he attends classes in the city."

Nadia grinned at Jessica as she spoke, her face lit up with her hand gestures all over the place as she described her date with Finn.

"Are you bringing him tonight?" Jessica asked.

"No, I thought tonight was just for the magazine people not plus ones. I've asked him to come with me on Saturday."

"Ah, that's great news. I can't wait to meet him. It's also fabulous that it's just business tonight, I don't have to look like a sad loner with no date. Who are you wearing?"

"I hate that expression," Nadia commented, wincing as she heard the words. "It sounds ridiculous, but I'm wearing Prada, a black slinky number. What about you?"

"A local designer has asked me to wear one of her dresses. It's bright red with a full skirt, but the top is a bit risky. The front and back is slit from neck to waist but with no skin showing. The pleats hide the secret until you stretch or someone slips their hand inside."

Jessica giggled at the prospect.

"Is that wishful thinking? Because if it is, I think you will find your handsome stranger this evening. He is going to be everything you want and need. My premonitions are never wrong. He will be running late so don't be disappointed if you don't meet him straight away," Nadia said.

"You do not have the gift of foresight, stop teasing me with glorious men and amazing sex, I can't cope," Jessica said, flopping down on the deck now that her sorbet cone was demolished.

"When we meet tomorrow to go through the clothes for the gala ball, I'll want to know all the details. Every last sordid one." Nadia said.

"Ok, if he does materialise, then you definitely have to bring Finn as your plus one on Saturday. If he is going to be living nearby, there is no excuse not to make a go of it. You don't usually have sex on a first date or the tenth, so he must have impressed you. Don't dismiss him as a would be boyfriend because you think he can't handle you travelling overseas all the time."

Nadia had used this excuse many times with Jessica. She assumed that no man would put up with her travelling away for weeks only to return for a few days and then go again. Jessica had been Nadia's mentor for a couple years, nurturing her in the ways of the fashion business.

"That's a deal. Now, I have to get going, I just dropped by to give you the lemony goodness. See you tonight."

Nadia left as silently as she arrived. She was always foreseeing people's love interests, but this time it was about Jessica. Each time Nadia talked about the next love interest, Jessica hoped that he would be for her, but she left the parties alone. Hopefully this time, her night will end differently.

Chapter 2

J essica Dockery hopped along the corridor from her kitchen to her living room, trying to put her red stiletto heels on. It didn't occur to her to stop for a moment and slip into them, she was running late and did everything at speed. Jessica's thoughts were still with Nadia from earlier in the day. Nadia's *beautiful body* brand was taking off, with the help of *Ipris* Magazine. Jessica was mentoring Nadia in the fashion business as a plus sized model. She too had been a plus sized super model for a decade. Fashion was a cut throat business, and when she started out, there was no one to mentor her. When she spotted Nadia in Jackson's Bay, she knew that Nadia was model perfect.

These days, Jessica attended a lot of fundraisers and parties, and that was what she was late for this evening. *Ipris* magazine's Editor-in-Chief had thrown a soiree for the people who were going to feature in the celebratory edition of the magazine. The annual gala ball was due to held in a few day's time. This evening was a smaller gathering with only two hundred guests attending. The champagne and cocktails party was a stand up an affair with very little to eat and too much to drink. A lethal combination for Jessica who couldn't hold her liquor.

After Nadia's meeting this morning, Jessica had eaten a large bowl of pasta in an attempt to line her stomach ready for the celebrations. The 140th Anniversary year for *Ipris* was a big deal in the industry. Many times there had been a danger that the publication would go under, but the owner Harvey Hinder had hired brilliant forward thinking editors who could drive the momentum forward. The ethos of the magazine, from the first publication back in 1887, was to empower women and their rights. The Hinder family, who had always owned the magazine, hired very smart women to run the editorial. Led by women for women who wanted the best in life and were willing to work for it.

Nadia had promised Jessica that she would meet the man of her dreams. Jessica had been on the lookout for Mr Right for the last year. She had stopped travelling the world and wanted to settle down. Jessica had been single for far too long, and her vibrator was becoming boring. She wanted the real thing. Preferably attached to a gentleman.

Snatching her keys from the sideboard next to her front door, she ran out of the door, slamming it behind her. Realising she'd forgotten her handbag, Jessica tutted and went back to her house to retrieve her bag and took a glance into the mirror to check everything was in place. Jessica twirled in front of the mirror to make sure the flared skirt of her dress hung properly.

The red dress had a high back and neckline. As she moved, Jessica checked that her breasts were well hidden. She couldn't wear a bra with the dress. The only way to know she wore nothing under the dress, was to part the material. Jessica hoped by the end of the night, it would be pulled apart like a pair of curtains by a tall, dark, handsome man, whose looks took her breath away.

The Imperial Estate was ten minutes walk from her house, up a steep hill and it had been raining heavily earlier. She hurried along the busy high street, hailing a taxi. She was an expert walking in stilettos, learned from her modelling days, and it stood her in good stead. She could stand, dance, and walk in high heels all day and all night. She loved the way it made her shapely legs look in her short dress. Her legs were her best feature, she would love to have handmade shoes, but the modelling industry didn't want to bestow expensive shoes on a hefty woman like her. She'd heard it time and time again. In all the years she'd won campaigns and had been booked over and over, none of them was for shoes. They said that her ankles weren't defined enough to show off their beautiful footwear. It was such a contentious issue that the top shoe designers had asked that she didn't wear their shoes to any events where she would be photographed.

Body shaming was the type of stigma that Jessica wanted to eradicate. She also hoped that her tall, dark, and handsome man didn't mind small breasts. Jessica couldn't care if the sex was for just one night, she needed the touch of a man's hands on her body. Preferably a man who knew what he was doing.

Jessica pushed through the brass edged revolving doors and into the foyer of the castle. She waved to the receptionist, her friend from her yoga class, and made her way to the ballroom at the back of the hotel. Jessica needed to climb the circular staircase and walk down a carpeted corridor. There was a sharp turn left and then another long corridor until she reached the double doors to the room hired for the fundraiser. The event had already started, and she was supposed to be meeting Rebecca Patterson, for a brief chat about Nadia.

"Wow, you can move fast on those heels," the deep male voice said behind her. Jessica prayed for two things, well three things. Handsome face, fit body, and no wedding ring. Turning slowly she checked his hand first. First tick. Then she glanced at his thighs that were large and looked firm in his tuxedo pants. Jessica would bet the first drink that he played rugby. Taking her time to assess his broad chest, hand tied bow tie and tanned throat, she urged her mind to check out his face. Three out of three.

Bingo.

"Years of practice, I can pretty do much anything in heels. What's your superpower?"

He raised his eyebrow and smirked.

"That would take a demonstration in a more private place than outside the doors of a party," he said.

The man stepped closer to Jessica, crowding her against the wall to the side of the main doors. She could feel the heat of his body as he leaned in and whispered in next to her ear. Jessica dipped her head to stop her lips from needing to press against his throat above his collar. In her five inch heels, she neared six feet. He slipped his arm around her waist, sliding a hand against her bare skin at the base of her back.

"We'll have to get this close, preferably closer. Dare you to find out what my super power might be?"

Jessica nodded, unable to utter a word. She inhaled his rich citrus aftershave that caused her heartbeat to race faster. The aroma aroused her senses. He smelled of peppery grapefruit. If they were alone in a room with a bed, she wouldn't have been able to trust her hands not to slowly undress him. He cupped her cheek with his other hand, making her raise her eyes to his.

"Is that a yes?" He asked quietly, his stare, holding her captive, willing her to say yes out loud.

"Yes, I dare to find out."

"Good. Tell me your name." He demanded. She narrowed her eyes at his tone, and he smirked his sexy smile.

"My name is Jessica, now tell me yours," she said, tilting her head mimicking his tone.

"Ramsay Holcroft. Now let's go to the party and have some fun. I haven't had an erection this hard in years. I want to get to know you a whole lot better before I take you to bed."

"You're a cocky bastard."

"Yes, I am. Come on, I'm late," he said.

Ramsay pulled away from her, dropped his gaze to her breasts and then to her shoes.

"Those are gorgeous heels," Ramsay said and held out his hand.

Jessica slipped her hand in his and grinned at him, the night had improved infinitely. He sidestepped to the double doors and was about to open them when they were pulled open.

"At last, you're here, thank you for coming Mr Holcroft, is this your wife?" The woman gushed as she reached to shake Ramsay's hand. "I'm Agatha, one of the many PAs," she blurted, shaking Jessica's hand. "I was tasked with finding you. We weren't sure if you were going to bring your wife this evening. It's lovely to meet you." Agatha stuck out her hand again to shake Jessica's hand, and she went along with it, looking up to Ramsay to question if he was married. "Ok, you have about twenty minutes until you need to give your speech, no more than ten minutes or they'll all head to the bar. Most of them are already hammered. Anyway, head to the stage at eight o'clock and I'll introduce you." Agatha said in a rush of words as she tapped frantically on her phone.

Agatha patted Ramsay's arm and then turned on her kitten heels and stalked back into the room. For a woman who looked to be in her late sixties, she was fast on her feet. They were left alone once more with the roar of laughter pouring out of the room.

"You're married?" Jessica asked in disbelief.

"No, I'm not married, never have been, never been close to it. I've no idea what she's talking about. The good part is, she will tell everyone you are my wife and that means you'll have to stay by my side all night." He grinned at her. "This event is not looking half as boring as I thought it would be."

Ramsay leaned across and kissed her cheek, taking her hand once more and leading her into the ballroom. He led her to the bar at the far end of the room. Jessica ordered a vodka and lemonade, then Ramsay ordered a neat whiskey. They fell silent while the barman poured their drinks. Jessica had no idea what to say. Nadia's premonition had come true, now that she had him and he was her husband for the night, she had no idea what to do with him. She hoped that he would take the lead and she could look forward to a passionate kiss at the end of the night.

"You'll need to stop licking your lips. I want to kiss them as it is, without you making them more inviting."

Jessica lifted her head to meet his eyes to find desire and a little fierceness. She dropped her eyes to his lips as he licked them.

"You just licked yours too," she murmured, gripping her glass, willing her hands to stay close to her body and not all over his.

"Are you saying that you want to kiss me, as much as I want to kiss you?"

"I think so, I can't think of anything else right now," she confessed, proud that she had told him and not denied it because Ramsay dipped his head and pressed his lips to hers. A feather light kiss, followed by a few more. She could taste a hint of whiskey on her lips as she licked them when he stood upright again.

"I hope that I don't scare you off and get to kiss you for longer later on," Ramsay said.

"I hope so too," she said.

It was the most honest sentence Jessica had uttered in a long time. She wanted him, there was no denying it.

Ramsay led Jessica by the elbow to the high tables. The small circular tables were at chest height and only big enough to rest a few glasses and a bowl of spiced nibbles. The room was filled with these tables, scattered about in no visible pattern. Jessica could see Rebecca over in the far corner speaking with a group of men. They made brief eye contact, long enough to send each other a heartfelt hello before they both resumed their attention to whom they were standing next to.

"I'm going to be tonight's auctioneer. Apparently, after my last attempt, Rebecca wanted me for her little party this evening." Jessica said.

"I'll buy whatever you're selling, just name your price," Ramsay said but didn't get to finish his tease.

Another PA for the magazine escorted her away to the side of the stage, handing her a stack of white cards. Jessica sifted through the words on the cards and nodded to the woman next to her. The PA gave her a microphone but told her to wait until the charity they were raising money for had been introduced.

Ramsay was the last person she expected to step up onto the stage to talk about the charity. He spoke passionately about the charity he headed. Jessica hadn't realised how fascinating getting fresh water to those who needed it in Africa was. He kept to his allotted ten minutes and then joined Jessica at the side of the stage.

"Knock 'em dead, darling, you're up," Ramsay said and kissed her soundly before moving through the crowd to get to their table.

Jessica hopped up the steps of the stage and strode across the empty floor a few times. His kiss had knocked her body temperature up a few degrees, and with the spotlights on her, she needed to get her act together. Jessica spoke eloquently about the auction, interspersing the seriousness of the charity's focus with jokes. She'd done her homework about the charity but didn't know the Ramsay she'd met, was the head of the charity. His name didn't appear on the website, only a handful of the trustees who had their pictures in different locations over in Africa.

The bidding started on the ten auction items with furious competition. The items were experiences that money couldn't buy unless you were super wealthy. The one thing that Jessica wanted was the handmade shoes. It was way out of her budget to bid, and reluctantly she pointed to the winner at the back of the room in the shadows. The woman had held up her white paddle each time the price bounced from her to another in the room.

An hour later, the charity auction had finished, and she was off the stage.

"You were amazing, I want you every year," Rebecca said and hugged her friend.

Rebecca had developed a firm friendship with Jessica the first time she met her. Jessica had pitched the idea of the plus sized model monthly feature in the magazine after she spotted Rebecca sitting opposite her on the tube, heading to Marylebone station.

"Now that I'm no longer modelling, my diary is completely empty, so I'm all yours," Rebecca said.

"You can still model, Jessica, you don't have to give that up," Rebecca chastised.

"I know, but I prefer the mentor side of modelling. Nadia is going to be a sensation, a world famous model, and she's all yours," Jessica said and clinked the edge of her water glass with Rebecca's.

"You found her, all credit to you. I just book her whenever I can. I can't believe she's only twenty-one, she seems so much older when you talk to her."

"She's too wise for me sometimes, but I love her anyway," Jessica said. "Good luck with the rest of the evening, I'll see you on Saturday, I hear there is going to be big announcements."

"Apparently so, but I have no idea what," Rebecca said and rolled her eyes.

Rebecca waved as she ascended the steps and spoke into the microphone, thanking Jessica's expert auction skills to raise thousands of pounds for their chosen charity.

Chapter 3

"I'm so glad you're my wife for the evening, I don't have to be auctioned off for the night," Ramsay said into her ear.

Jessica pulled a five-pound note out of her purse and slipped it along the table cloth to Ramsay.

"That's my bid, I hope I get my money's worth," she said.

"That depends on what you expect for a fiver."

"You said that you would show me your super power and that we would need to get real close," she said.

She didn't know if it was the desperation of wanting sex with this man, or that she hadn't had sex in a year that drove her shameless flirting. Either way, Ramsay had told her that he would take her to bed, so she decided to believe him and enjoy the foreplay.

"I'll show you if you'll let me. Are you single?"

"Yes," she said, staring at him straight in the eye.

When the speeches had finished, the DJ started playing 70s disco music. Most of the people stayed where they were, chatting around the tall tables to mingle with the party guests. Jessica looked around at the guests in their beautiful clothes. For a moment, she wondered why she was there at all. Jessica hadn't done a shoot for six months. Her time was spent scouting for the model agency she was assigned to.

She turned full circle back to Ramsay's face to find his lips an inch from hers. She could feel his warm breath on her face. His arm had moved up and around her waist. He gently stroked his thumb on her back.

"Who makes your shoes?" Ramsay asked.

"They're from a high street store, I imagine they're made in a factory overseas," Jessica said and took a glance at her red heels.

Ramsay led them to the seats at the side of the room and sat down. Jessica sat next to him and crossed her legs, teasing him with her legs brushing against his.

"Your feet should be in bespoke shoes that are only made for you," Ramsay dropped his hand to her calf and traced his fingertips up to Jessica's knee.

"I'd sell a kidney for one of a kind shoes. They could have both to be fair, it's a shame *Ipris* didn't accept organs as payment because I really wanted to bid on that auction prize."

Ramsay laughed hard, a few of the guests turned. His laugh was contagious, and a few nearby observers started to giggle.

"What's so funny?"

"You have no idea who I am, do you?"

"I know your name, but that's about it. We've talked nonsense for most of the evening. Talking about work stuff can wait."

"I want to kiss you again," Ramsay said.

"You want to kiss me in front of all these people?" Jessica asked. There had to be people in the room that knew he wasn't married. There had to be women in this room that had their eyes set on the handsome man who was asking her for another kiss.

"Well, technically you are my wife so it wouldn't be truly outrageous for me to kiss you," he said.

"Then go right ahead, husband, kiss me," she said.

He did once he'd pulled her to her feet.

Ramsay's arm pulled her closer, holding fast to her waist. He kissed her with restraint, resisting the urge to lay her across the table and devour every inch of her body. Ramsay held the back of her neck to push his tongue into her open mouth. That first touch of her warm, wet tongue, had his cock pulsing. She tasted of merlot wine and red lipstick. He wanted to suck hard on her neck, marking her as his for the night. She clutched at his neck, digging her fingernails into his skin. Her soft hands were around his throat, gently squeezing as she kissed him back.

Pulling away, Ramsay desperately tried to gain control of his breathing and his hard cock. He looked at her face, taking in her glassy eyes. She looked drunk on lust. He thought he might cry if she wouldn't let him fuck her that evening.

"Was that my kiss goodnight?" She whispered, looking at his lips and holding firm to his neck.

"I hope not. I pray that you'll let me kiss you again," Ramsay begged. He'd never asked a woman for a kiss before.

"I want you to take me home, to kiss me goodnight when the sun comes up. I'm hoping that we wouldn't have had any sleep. That we're exhausted, tangled in my crumpled bed sheets." Jessica said.

Ramsay couldn't believe what he was hearing. This beautiful woman who made his heart beat out of his chest wanted him.

"Let's go, my car is outside," Ramsay said and stood to take her with him. "Did you bring a coat?"

"No, I'm ready to go. I don't live that far away, we could walk," she suggested.

Ramsay hadn't walked with a woman for a hell of a long time, he'd had plenty of short relationships, but there wasn't any romance involved. Walking hand in hand with Jessica seemed the best thing in the world to do. Ramsay hadn't been back to Jackson's Bay since the last charity ball. He wondered if the secluded spot on the beach was still there. When Ramsay was in his late teens, he would make out with the girls at the end of the beach on the sand dunes. He did like the vision of getting wrapped up in Jessica's bed sheets more than getting sand in all the wrong places.

As he moved through the tipsy party goers, holding Jessica's hand, he nodded his goodbyes to the men and women as he passed. Anxious to get out of the castle as soon as he could, he tugged Jessica along. She kept pace with him, eager to leave too.

By the time they reached the top of the staircase, they were running down the stairs and through the lobby. Their laughter causing people to turn their heads to the happy couple.

As soon as they reached the pavement outside, Ramsay grabbed Jessica and fiercely kissed her. He pulled her hair to expose her neck, pressing his open mouth against her skin, up and down the column of her throat.

"Damn it, Jessica, you've turned me into a starving man. I don't think I can walk, we need to get to your place, now."

Chapter 4

He didn't wait for her to answer and pulled her along the pavement to his waiting car. He'd sent a text to his driver as soon as Jessica had agreed to leave the party. Ramsay opened the back door to help Jessica into the car and then joined her on the other side. He pulled her onto his lap, spreading the material of her dress apart at her cleavage. Grabbing her breasts roughly, he took one hard nipple into his mouth, sucking and biting until Jessica pulled at his hair.

"Where do you live, I need to tell the driver," he said in between kissing her mouth and her neck.

Jessica turned to speak to the driver, who nodded and pulled away from the parking spot.

"Are you sure about this, we've only just met? We're taking this fake marriage a little too far aren't we?" Jessica said, leaning back on Ramsay's knees. She fixed her dress and laughed when Ramsay pouted because he couldn't see her breasts anymore.

"Oh hell yes, I'm sure. You're stunning, funny, smart, and my heart hasn't raced this fast when I've kissed a girl in a hell of a long time. Plus, you can do anything in heels."

"I'm so glad I met you this evening, I almost didn't come. My friend persuaded me, telling me that I'd meet a handsome man that would sweep me off my feet," Jessica said and rolled her eyes at Nadia's promise.

"I can sweep you off your feet and carry you to your bed-room, we've arrived," Ramsay said, pushing his fingers through her hair to capture her lips in a soft kiss.

Jessica hadn't realised that they'd stopped moving. She moved from his lap to the seat next to him and dropped her hands to her lap as she stared out of the window. Ramsay thought that she was having second thoughts, and his heart fell to his stomach.

"What's wrong?" Ramsay asked her after a minute had passed.

"I'm sorry, I've invited you back, and I think my bedroom looks like a bomb has hit it. I don't usually bring men back to my place."

Ramsay laughed at her confession, glad that it was a trivial worry.

"We can go back to the hotel. I have a room there," he suggested and took Jessica's hand.

"No, I want you in my bed. Can you come in with me but stay in the living room and let me clear up?"

"I'll wait as long as you want Jessica. I have a feeling it will be worth it," Ramsay said.

Jessica got out of the car while Ramsay spoke to his driver. He joined her on the pavement outside her house, and they watched the car drive away in silence. It was still early, little after ten in the evening. Jessica took her keys from her purse and opened her bright red front door.

As soon as the front door was closed, Ramsay moved Jessica to the wall and pressed his large body against hers. He took his time to stroke her throat with his thumbs until he kissed her. Hard, punishing kisses, his lips firmly capturing hers, moulding his mouth to hers. She managed to break away and take a few shallow breaths.

"I need to get you naked, but I need to clear my bed. Stay here and count to sixty seconds then come up. It's the door straight ahead at the top of the stairs."

Jessica ran up the stairs in her heels checking when she reached the top to make sure he was where she left him. He undid his bow tie, slowly pulling on one end as he stared at her. One hand in his trousers pocket as he loosened the material. He threw it to the floor and undid his top button.

"I'm at thirty seconds," he said and smirked.

"Don't take any more clothes off. You are the most erotic sight I have ever seen standing at the bottom of my stairs, taking off your tie. I want to see the rest."

Jessica moved into her bedroom clearing off the clothes that were still on their hangers and hastily stuffed them back in her wardrobe. Her bed was made underneath the clothing, all she needed to do was kick a few pairs of shoes under her bed. Jessica had her back to the door. Just as the last shoe disappeared out of sight, he was invading her space. He kissed her shoulder while a hand sneaked inside her dress to tweak her nipple.

Twisting in his arms, she faced him for a kiss. She laughed when she saw his bow tie perfectly tied at his neck.

"You spoil me, Ramsay, will you undress for me?" Jessica asked.

"Your wish is my command," he said. "First, I want to take this dress off you. Then you can relax on the bed to watch the show."

She turned her back and lifted her hair around her shoulder, allowing it to drape over her breast. Ramsay's feather like touches on her nape made her needy for his firm touch. The hairs stood out on her arms, desire tingled down her spine as he pulled down the zip of her dress. The material pooled at her feet, and she stepped to one side. Bending down to pick up her dress, she heard Ramsay moan. When she stood, he brought his palm over her bottom, hooking his fingers into her sheer red knickers. It was his turn to crouch when he pulled her underwear down to her ankles. She stepped aside once more and out of her shoes.

Ramsay positioned her body to face his. With his hands on her hips, he kissed her again. Jessica leaned against his body with her hands squeezing his firm arse. His kisses made her wet with desire, there was nothing calm about her heartbeat or the heat spreading from her core to her fingertips. Curling her toes, Jessica brought her hands to his belt buckle. She needed him naked and couldn't care about his strip tease. Ramsay got the message and undressed while they kissed. He gave up the battle of trying to help and held her face while she pulled his shirt from his trousers and unbuttoned the material. She pushed his jacket and shirt off at the same time, once his bow tie was undone.

Circling around to his back, Jessica unbuttoned his trousers and pulled down the zip. She pushed his pants down along with his boxer shorts. She wasn't ready to see his cock but wanted to feel his hardness first. She followed as he stepped out of his trousers and found a free space on the carpet to stand.

"You're a good-looking man, if this is only one night then I want to make the most of it," Jessica said.

She kissed his back, trailing her fingertips over his stomach and hip bones. Taking his erection in her hand, she groaned at the size of his large, hard cock. Her fantasy was coming true.

"Fuck this, Jessica, your teasing is too much. I need to slide inside you in the next two minutes, or I'll come all over your hand. Get on the bed."

She squeezed his cock once more and crawled onto the bed, pushing the duvet to the base of the bed with her feet. The metal posts keeping it on the bed. Jessica grabbed the box of condoms from her bedside drawer and balanced them on the pillow next to her.

Ramsay smirked, gripping his erection in his hand, slowly stroking and taming his impending orgasm. He drank in the sight of Jessica lying on the bed. Her neatly shaved pussy teasing him to come closer, tantalising him to slide inside and feel her muscles grip his cock. He denied contact for a minute longer as he stilled his hand at the crown, pressing hard to calm his need to fuck her.

It wasn't working, he wanted to fuck Jessica. Her open mouth and rising chest invited him to abandon all hope of lasting more than three minutes before he came.

"Can we have a quickie now and then spend the rest of the night taking our time?" Ramsay asked, his voice breaking when she spread her legs to play with her clit. "Stop doing that, I'm going to come if I have to watch you masturbate."

"What would you like me to do?" Jessica asked and raised her hands to tuck them behind her head.

Ramsay lay on his back and pulled Jessica to straddle his hips. He gave her the box of condoms and invited her to sheath him. He wanted further punishment of her hands on his body, to test his will.

"Hurry, Jessica, just hurry," he said.

Jessica covered his cock and shifted forward, positioning him at the entrance to her wet core. He wrapped one arm around her waist to bring her down to his chest, and another hand grabbed her arse cheek to keep her in place. He raised his hips in one fluid hard thrust and entered her body. Jessica let out a long moan. She hung onto his neck while he fucked her like his life depended on her reaching an orgasm before he did. Her mouth was stretched wide, her neck pulled back as much as he'd let her move. Ramsay bit and kissed the column of her neck as he slapped his thighs against her arse. Jessica pushed her knees against his hips, tensing all of her muscles as he sped up his thrusts. By the time Ramsay reached his orgasm, Jessica was yelling in ecstasy when she tipped over into oblivion. The throbs of her orgasm stuttering as her muscles tried to ripple over Ramsay's large cock inside her. It was almost painful to let her orgasm carry on, but she relaxed in his arms and rested her cheek on his chest. She could feel his heart hammering at a startling speed as he hugged her close.

"I've never come that hard before, what is this witchery you have cast over me?" Ramsay asked once he'd caught his breath and kissed her forehead.

"It's *you* that's cast the spell over *me*. You've ruined me for any other man, is that your super power?" Jessica replied.

"My superpower is handmade shoes. I'm a shoe designer, I make bespoke shoes for women. But if fucking you to orgasm is a superpower, I won't complain."

Jessica nearly wept at the news of his profession, she never wanted to let him leave her bedroom. A man who knew how to fuck and make shoes was heaven sent. Nadia's prediction was spot on.

"I'm chaining you to this bed, you are not leaving," Jessica whispered into his ear.

"Sounds perfect, but first I want to explore every inch of your body."

Chapter 5

J essica waited on the train platform with a coffee in her hand. She'd decided to take a last minute trip to London. Her agency had called to see if she would go and visit a photo shoot for a model called Bernice. They were thinking of taking her on their books. Reports had come back to them that she was a lot to handle. Her boss had asked her to check her out on a job.

Ramsay had left her early to get a start on his day but promised to call her later. She was deliciously sore from her night with Ramsay, who confessed that he played rugby on the odd weekend he was in the city. He had a house in London and also his ancestral home in Jackson's Bay. While she lay against his chest munching on buttered toast, he told her about his shoe business.

She loved the way he spoke about his passion for shoes. Her jealousy of all those women that had his bespoke shoes in their wardrobes bubbled to the surface when she huffed at his commentary. He never made the same shoe twice, allowing the wealthy to have whatever they wanted to match their dresses.

The brogues she wore for her trip to London were comfortable. Rushing around London was not a job for heels, especially when she wasn't going on a go see. The train rattled into the station, blowing stray papers along and up into the air. Jessica got on the last carriage and settled herself into first class. Lifting her laptop out of her satchel, she hooked up to the wifi and began researching Bernice. Her social media was full of photos of her at parties in London, numerous pictures of her with other women and a glass of wine in her hand. Her poses were camera ready. Her waif thin frame, perfectly positioned to show off long legs. Bernice had made Instagram her slave. Over a million followers for an unsigned model was an epic milestone. Jessica clicked through to Bernice's website. The portfolio she'd put together was professional. On the surface, everything was going for her, except it was all too calculated, too perfect. Jessica would like to have seen some evidence of imperfection, but there were none.

A text drew her away from the young girl on her screen.

Ramsay: What are you doing?

Jessica: I'm on my way to London

Ramsay: That's a shame. I wanted to take you to lunch.

Jessica: I'm free tomorrow

Ramsay: How about dinner tonight?

Jessica: I won't be back until very late

Ramsay: Are you avoiding me?

Jessica dialled his number, she couldn't bear the thought that he was feeling rejected and she wanted to hear his voice.

"Hi," he answered on the second ring.

"Hey, handsome. I'm not avoiding you. I took a last minute job with my agency to check out a model, but by all accounts, she's a diva."

"Good. I would hate to think that you'd changed your mind about me. I need to convince you to go to the *Ipris* Gala with me as my date."

Jessica smiled at the phone, she wanted to go with him to every party.

"You don't have to convince me. I'd love to go with you," Jessica said.

"Why can't I see you tonight?"

"I won't be back until midnight, I won't be able to keep my eyes open. These types of days, rushing across London tires me out. I wouldn't be very good company."

"I'm sure you'd be delightful company, but I understand. Shall I pick you up in the morning? I have somewhere I want to show you. I think you'll like it. I had a whole day planned to lure you into being my date, and now that's all ruined."

She could hear his pout, and she laughed.

"I don't play games, Ramsay. I like you and would love to see you again. Pick me up at ten tomorrow, and I can rescind my acceptance so you can do your wooing."

"Just to be clear though you are coming with me," he asked.

"Such a fool, I'll see you tomorrow. If I don't have the perfect day then the deal is off," she said.

Jessica never knew how to play hard to get, if she liked a man she told him. Most of the time it made them run the other way, but she suspected that Ramsay was different. She thought that Ramsay liked her a lot.

"I'll see you tomorrow, beautiful. Kick ass today," Ramsay said and ended the call.

She tucked the phone into her satchel and packed up her laptop. She'd learned as much as she needed to about Bernice, she looked forward to meeting the young woman at the photo shoot. Jessica made a quick call to the photographer and make-up team that was covering the high street clothing advert to check a few details. They knew she would be there, but Bernice didn't.

Chapter 6

The next morning, Jessica swung her bare feet back and forth while she waited for Ramsay to come back. She had hopped up onto the workbench when Ramsay had kneeled down in front of her. He wanted to get a closer look at her feet. Commenting on her sparkly purple painted toe nails, Ramsay also asked her what colour dress she would be wearing to the *Ipris* Gala. When she answered black, he sighed dramatically but didn't make any further comment.

Quizzing her further on the colour of her handbag and jewellery, he found out that everything she would be wearing was black. He could work with black, but he was hoping for a splash of colour. He had the morning to make her a handmade pair of shoes. Plenty of time. His brother had kept the room where he started his business exactly how he left it. There wasn't a speck of dust anywhere. His supply cupboard was stocked with materials needed for shoe making. It had been years since he'd used this studio but was grateful that his brother had hoped he would return to the family home to live.

He'd picked Jessica up at her house an hour ago. They'd arrived at the workshop without seeing another soul. Jessica had spent the entire journey from the driveway, through the corridors, and into the workshop with her head up. She couldn't get enough of the architecture of the building, especially the gargoyles spying her over their perch above the main door.

Jessica had a childhood fascination about the stone statues, making up stories with her brother about what they did when their backs were turned. She thought they were mischievous, making faces while dancing on their plinths.

The smell of coffee had hit her senses before she saw Ramsay come into the room. He was chatting animatedly with another man and woman as he approached. Jumping down from the bench, she approached the couple. She stood stock still when she caught sight of the man.

"Oh fuck," she muttered.

Loudly it seemed when the man laughed. He gave her a wink and stretched his hand out. Jessica shook his hand, opening and closing her mouth, starting at Ramsay. She glanced back from Ramsay to the woman and shook her hand too.

"I'm sorry, forgive my bad language, I'm taken by surprise. I did the same when I met Bono," Jessica rambled.

"I'm Harvey, and this is my girlfriend, Ingrid," Harvey said by way of introduction. Harvey placed his hand at the base of Ingrid's back and stood close to her.

"I know who you are. You own *Ipris*. I'm staggered that I'm standing so close to you, I thought you were myth and legend."

"I like her, Ramsay, I like her a lot. Honesty is a beautiful trait," Harvey said.

Harvey slapped Ramsay on the back who was trying to stifle his laughter, as was Ingrid.

"You'd have to be living under a rock to not know who you are too, Jessica. I admire you and your intensity to remove the stigma of categorising women based on their figure. Some amazing women are writing and working at the magazine. I wish I could find the time to meet them all, but my time is limited."

"I understand. It's great to meet you, are you going to the gala on Saturday? I hear you've never been to any of them," Jessica said.

She winced at her honest question. Ramsay slung an arm around her shoulder and pulled her in for a kiss on her temple.

"Yes, brother, why don't you come on Saturday, you can prove that you exist and not the big bad ogre the town, company, and industry think you are."

"You're his brother?" Jessica said, clamping her hand over her mouth when she realised her screeching question.

"Yeah, he's my big brother, and this is our house. Although the town thinks we only bought it a few years ago." Ramsay confirmed.

A minute of silence followed while Jessica processed that she was standing in front of the owner of *Ipris*, the magazine she worked for. The magazine she had graced the cover twice in her ten-year career.

"If I can persuade my girlfriend to come with me, I will attend the gala. No guarantees for how long, but I will turn up. If she says yes," Harvey said, pointing his thumb at Ingrid.

"I'm already going, Rebecca invited me," Ingrid confessed.

Harvey stood back for a moment and looked at Ingrid, squinting his eyes to read her mind. "Of course she did. Interesting, very interesting. Does that mean we are going as a couple?" Harvey asked, blotting out that Ramsay and Jessica were waiting for Ingrid's answer.

"If that makes you happy, then yes, I'll be glad to be your date," Ingrid said.

Harvey grabbed her hand and kissed her palm.

"It was lovely to meet you, Jessica, make sure he takes care of you, and we'll see you for dinner tonight," Harvey said.

He left the room with Ingrid jogging behind his long stride. She called out her goodbye through her laugh at Harvey and his urgency to exit the room.

"Their relationship is recent, they're still in the honeymoon phase."

"Dinner? I'm staying for dinner? I don't have a thing to wear," Jessica said. She looked down at her dress, inspecting it for creases.

"I can drop you back to get changed if you really want to, but it will be a casual dinner. You look lovely as you are. Make the decision later, once we're done with your shoes."

"You're going to make me some shoes?"

"Yup," he said.

Ramsay helped her back up onto the bench, taking her calf in his hand.

"Well fuck, I think I might cry," she said.

"Don't cry, my sweet. I'll make you some shoes for tomorrow night, we'll have dinner. If I'm lucky, I might get to see you naked in between the two."

"All right. I'll try not to speak my mind at dinner. Meeting people like Harvey transforms me into a gibbering wreck."

"You must have met hundreds of mega famous people in your job." Ramsay was concentrating on her toes, massaging the tiny bones, getting used to her shape.

"And I made a fool of myself in front of every single one. I am known for it. Only a few were offended by my candid questions."

"I can tell you that Harvey liked you. He doesn't socialise very often. He prefers to run the family empire from behind a computer screen. He has a team of trusted men and women who are the face of the publishing business."

"Why don't you run the business with him?"

"Candid?"

"Yeah, sorry," Jessica said.

She tried to inch away, but Ramsay held onto her ankle.

"You can ask me anything you want, I won't get offended," he said. "I don't like the business side, magazines or newspapers. I have always wanted to design women's shoes. I'm fascinated by the way women's heels cause their hips to sway as they walk. My mother loved her shoes, she had shelves of them. My father bought her a pair every month that they were married. They'd go shopping together, sometimes he would choose and sometimes she did. It made her happy, and he would have done anything to see a smile on her face. They had a great marriage, I envied them."

"You've a romantic heart, Ramsay. I love that," she said.

Harvey's easy nature with Jessica settled Harvey's nerves. Usually, he would be stressed introducing a woman to his brother, but with Jessica, it felt natural. He let go of her calf and then pulled over a stool on wheels. Ramsay got to work with making the cast of her feet.

"I'm going to make you black patent, peep toe stiletto shoes. Does that please you, madam?" Ramsay asked as he massaged her feet with the cream he'd squeezed from a tube.

"Absolutely, I will treasure them forever. Does this mean I owe you a kidney?"

"You owe me nothing. For months until I saw you at the *Ipris* soiree, I had lost the desire to make shoes, to design shoes. You are my muse. I want to make you a wardrobe full of shoes to go with every outfit you have. Once I make the cast, I'll be able to do that. I have so many designs running around my head, and all of them have you walking down a Paris catwalk. Your long, beautiful legs showing off the heels I'll make, with you in mind."

Ramsay spoke so eloquently that Jessica didn't interrupt him. While he was talking, he measured and moulded plaster around her feet. Once that part was finished, he moved onto designing the shoe on his laptop while it set. Jessica wanted a unique symbol stamped on the sole so they would be forever just for her. Once the pattern was cut, Ramsay got to work. He zoned out for a few hours concentrating on his shoe. The housekeeper brought in a tray of sandwiches and a pot of coffee. Ramsay didn't want to break, so Jessica ate alone, just outside the doors of the studio on a lounger. The enormous pool glistened in the sunshine with an inflatable bed drifting up and down the pool by the jets underneath the surface.

Ramsay had given her his laptop so that she could do her work while she waited and came to apologise to her every hour for neglecting her. She waved him away, delighted that she would gain a pair of shoes from the afternoon's work.

It was close to six when he came back out with his hands behind his back. Jessica looked up when Ramsay approached and grinned. He matched her smile and brought the pair of shoes around to his waist so that she could see.

"They're gorgeous," Jessica half whispered and half shouted. She leapt up from the lounger and hugged Ramsay, wrapping her arms around his neck. She kissed his cheek, his neck and then his mouth.

"Can I try them on?" She asked after she'd finished kissing him.

"I want to fuck you in just these," he said.

Ramsay crouched and put them on the floor. Jessica was silenced at his request, her heart pounding hard at the thought of being bent over a table and fucked by this man.

"You want to fuck me in these. Now?"

"Yes, now," he answered.

She picked up the shoes, her feet still bare from the many fittings of the cast and pattern. Ramsay lifted her into his arms and carried her to the pool house. Using his elbow to push down the handle, he took her into the living room and then into the bedroom at the back. Ramsay deposited her on the vanity unit in the bathroom and pointed a single finger at her. She nodded and held onto the heels of her new shoes, waiting for his return.

Ramsay went to lock the doors and pull the duvet off the bed. By the time he returned to the bathroom, he was naked and hard. Jessica's eyes darted to his erection and then to his face. Ramsay pulled her to a standing position, lifted her dress over her head, and removed her lingerie just as quickly.

"Put your shoes on," Ramsay told her.

Jessica placed the shoes on the floor and turned her back to Ramsay. She caught his eye in the mirror while using the vanity table top to balance as she slipped her feet into her shoes. She sighed aloud while her feet settled into the perfectly fitted shoes. She groaned as she wiggled her painted toes.

"Bend over," Ramsay said and pushed gently on her back.

Jessica grabbed the neck of each water tap and bent at the waist. Ramsay stood behind her, nudging his erection against her arse cheek. Placing one foot in between hers, he kicked her feet apart. Jessica was expecting her legs to be parted wide, but the thrill of being commanded accelerated her building orgasm. An involuntary throb cascaded down her pussy walls, and an exclamation left her lips. Ramsay swiped his fingers through her wet pussy lips and slid inside, he kept doing that until she looked up.

"Keep looking and hold on tight," Ramsay said.

His cock was ready to slip inside her body, just his sheathed tip nudged in. He wrapped her long hair around his wrist and grabbed hold of her hip with the other hand. His concentration was on her arse. He watched as his cock entered her body, slowly and deliberately. When he was fully inside her pussy, he looked at the mirror. Jessica was drunk on lust, fixated on his face, white knuckles showing as she held on. With a slow blink, Ramsay pulled out and then slammed back inside. He witnessed Jessica's eyes roll to the back of her head, and her knees lock into place. Holding on hard, his fingers dug into her fleshy hip. He let go of her hair and held onto her other hip. Jessica's breasts swayed violently, and he fucked her hard. Flesh slapping against skin, the echoes bouncing off the tiled walls of the bathroom. His grunts and her moans blended as one until their orgasms took them over. Ramsay came first with an anguished cry. Jessica's orgasm came a minute later when Ramsay stroked her wet clit with feather like touches. She detonated around his cock, hundreds of tiny spasms grabbing hold of his erection.

He hugged her, leaning over her body as she flattened against the cold surface of the cupboard. Her face to the side as she regained her faculties.

"You're so strong. I was lost to the passion," Jessica muttered.

"Did I hurt you?" Ramsay said.

He stood up and slipped from her body. Turning her, he saw her small, shy smile as her arms wrapped around his waist.

"No, you didn't hurt me, I loved it. The perfect way to christen these shoes, don't you think?"

"I couldn't agree more."

Ramsay picked her up again and took her over to the bed. They cuddled together, not needing the duvet but just the single sheet to cover them.

"We have a couple of hours before dinner, do you want to stay here or go back and change?" Ramsay asked.

"I don't want to move from this position until I absolutely have to," she answered.

"Good answer."

Chapter 7

After they had shared a shower, Jessica got dressed and refused to take her shoes off. She claimed that she needed to break them in ready for the *Ipris* Gala. Ramsay was thrilled that she was wearing his creation. It had been a while since he'd worked in his studio by himself to create a bespoke pair for a beautiful woman. He'd carved a one sided silhouette of a curvaceous woman on the bottom of the shoe just before the curve of the heel as a mark that these shoes were hers and hers alone. Ramsay stood in the pool house watching Jessica parade up and down next to the pool showing Ingrid her shoes. At one point, Jessica slipped them off and let Ingrid try them on. It appeared they were the same shoe size as Ingrid did the catwalk along the pool. He glimpsed Harvey on the other side of the pool in the drawing room looking through the window at Ingrid, smiling. Ramsay caught his eye and nodded. At the same time, they exited and walked towards their women.

A selection of cocktails were on a tray in between the loungers, Ingrid and Jessica talked like they'd already had half a dozen. Their animated chatter was lost on the men who talked business briefly and then listened to Jessica talk about the young woman she'd met the previous day.

"The problem is, she thinks that everyone should love her," Jessica said. "Bernice has all the glamour and grace you could want in a model but lacks any diplomacy. She naturally rubs people up the wrong way. I just don't know if she does it deliberately or is oblivious."

"What's her name?" Harvey asked.

"Bernice Drake," Jessica answered after a large sip of her martini. "Have you heard her name?"

"No, can't say I have. Did you get a chance to talk to her, find out how she ticks?" Ramsay asked sitting next to her on the lounger.

Harvey sat next to Ingrid nursing a cold bottle of beer.

"I spent time talking to her when she had her hair and makeup done. A lot of the time, she was pouting at her phone while she took a picture for her Insta account while dodging my questions. One minute I was asking what kind of model she wanted to be and the next she was asking why I'd given up on modelling and let myself go."

"I didn't take the bait. I smiled and laughed, and tried a different angle to get her to talk, but veiled insults were her weapon. She aimed them at her hair stylist, asking when he was going to get his qualification."

"Sound like trouble to me, I wouldn't book her for a shoe shoot," Ramsay said.

"I have to agree there, I wouldn't want her to represent the magazine. A nasty attitude spreads like wildfire, passive aggressive women are the worst kind." Harvey pointed out.

"My gut is saying to stay clear, let another agency have her if they want. The dilemma is, when she's in front of the camera she takes direction. The shoot was done in half the time it would usually take for a novice."

"She may be able to get the shot first time, but if her brand is toxic, that will outweigh her perfect pose. Give her a miss is my advice, there are hundreds of beautiful women who want to model and are professional too. You'll find another," Harvey said.

Jessica relaxed about her problem for the first time since she'd woken. Bernice's attitude had bothered her, and she couldn't wait to get away from the woman. The tiny verbal jabs took their toll, and by the time she had said goodbye after a late supper, Jessica was exhausted from telling Bernice what she thought of her.

"She's coming to the Gala tomorrow, I have no idea how she got an invitation, and she wasn't telling me who had invited her. I guess we'll find out tomorrow." Jessica said.

"I think tomorrow is going to be one massive explosion of one upmanship. Rumour has it a rock star is going to reveal a big secret, and an actress is going to gatecrash. For my first *Ipris* Gala, I'm going to be entertained all evening." Harvey said, he raised his bottle to clink glasses with everyone. "Let's the celebrations begin," he toasted.

"Let's eat," Ramsay said when he spotted the housekeeper lingering in the side doorway to the mansion.

About the Author

Thank you for reading Sunshine and Lightning, I can't tell you how happy it makes me that you spent the time reading it. On the next page is the first chapter of book two, High Heels and Summer Mornings. We get to know Ingrid Stellar and Harvey Hinder, plus a few more guests for the *Ipris* gala. If you want to skip to the end and find out what happens at the party of the year, then Flashbulbs and Champagne reveals how all the characters end up.

I have a group on Facebook called Grace Harper Books where I share news first about covers and excerpts. You can also find me on the following social media.
Instagram: @GraceHarperBooks
Facebook Page: @GraceHarperBooks
Email: authorgraceharper@gmail.com
Website: www.graceharperbooks.com

Other titles by Grace Harper:

<u>Red & Black Series</u>
Charcoal Notes
Crimson Melodies
raven acoustics
cardinal lyrics
Onyx Keys
vermillion chords
<u>A Standalone Novel</u>
The Stranger's Voice
<u>A Standalone Novella</u>
Stranded at New Year
His christmas surprise

Printed in Great Britain
by Amazon

38724893R00066